SHADOW OF DEATH

Books by Angela Roquet

Return to Limbo City (A Lana Harvey Spin-off Series)
Life After Death
Shadow of Death
Death's Door (Summer 2022)
Tree of Death (Autumn 2022)
To the Death (Winter 2022)

Lana Harvey, Reapers Inc.
Graveyard Shift
Pocket Full of Posies
For the Birds
Psychopomp
Death Wish
Ghost Market
Hellfire and Brimstone
Limbo City Lights (short story collection)
The Illustrated Guide to Limbo City

Blood Vice
Blood Vice
Blood and Thunder
Blood in the Water
Blood Dolls
Thicker Than Blood
Blood, Sweat, and Tears
Flesh and Blood
Out for Blood

Spero Heights
Blood Moon
Death at First Sight
The Midnight District

Visit **angelaroquet.com** for a complete list of Angela's works.

SHADOW OF DEATH

BOOK TWO OF
RETURN TO LIMBO CITY

ANGELA ROQUET

VIOLENT SIREN PRESS

SHADOW OF DEATH

Copyright © 2022 by Angela Roquet

www.angelaroquet.com

Cover Art by Rebecca Frank

ISBN: 978-1-951603-34-2

For Paul and Xavier,
the center of my universe.

CHAPTER ONE

*"I believe that if life gives you lemons, you should
make lemonade… And try to find somebody whose life
has given them vodka, and have a party."*
—Ron White

SHOPPING IN HELL was a unique experience. Occasionally, Bub took me to Lilith Enchanted, an overpriced dress boutique. But he knew my dress size and what I liked—or rather, what *he* liked and what I would tolerate—so most of the gowns I owned arrived in fancy black boxes embossed with the boutique's serpent-entwined apple logo.

The other stores and businesses were hit or miss. Mostly miss. I didn't need any horn bling or fancy oils for a spaded tail. No hellfire facials or talon buffing. And the thought of drinking a smoothie that consisted of tears from seven deadly sinners almost made me throw up in my mouth.

But Tasha Henry couldn't exactly meet me in Limbo City where she was wanted for crimes against Eternity. Her ransom deal with the Hell Committee had included immunity and citizenship in the only afterlife they had the authority to grant it. She also had enough coin in her coffers to keep her comfortable for a century. Or at least a few decades, considering how quickly she appeared to be blowing through it.

Of course, I couldn't bring myself to scold her for the devil-may-care spending while admiring the new boots she'd gifted me as a peace offering.

"Those are to say thank you for the hot tip," Tasha explained as I zipped the leather sheaths up my calves. "I'm not apologizing, because I'm not sorry."

"Duly noted." I tried to smile but it felt more like a cringe.

Being this big of a sucker for a sweet pair of kicks was embarrassing, but it was a vice I shared with Tasha. She sported a matching pair of the stiletto boots in red. Mine were an oily black that went nicely with the leather jacket I was still wearing since I'd expected this meeting to go south before it even began. Not so south that we'd come down to blows—we were in public, after all—but I certainly hadn't expected to linger long enough outside the Salome Bistro to have brunch with the exiled reaper who'd double-crossed me.

A horned waitress stopped at our table and began unloading a serving tray with an order I assumed Tasha had placed before I'd arrived. "Two pomegranate mimosas with deviled crab omelets, plus a forbidden fruit and flesh platter. Can I get you ladies anything else?" the waitress chirped.

"I think we're good for now," Tasha answered then turned back to me. "I ordered for us both since you were running late."

"I wasn't late. *You* were early."

"Nuance." Tasha shrugged and took a sip of her mimosa. Her shoulders had gradually relaxed after I'd accepted the boots instead of flipping over the wrought-iron table and storming off down Gula Boulevard. And while there was certainly no honey in her tongue, it wasn't quite as razor sharp as I was used to either. There was another shoe somewhere—a figurative shoe, considering I was wearing the literal ones—and it was sure to drop soon.

In the meantime, I eyed the juicy spread laid out between us and tried not to drool on myself. I'd been too uptight about our meeting to bother with breakfast, and now it was nearly lunchtime. I supposed it wouldn't hurt to have a bite or two while I waited for the plot to thicken.

"So, what have you been doing with yourself?" I asked as I forked a slice of bacon off the fruit and flesh platter. "You know, besides lavishing in the spoils of your betrayal."

Tasha snorted. "Betrayal implies we had some pact or sworn loyalty to one another, which we did not."

"There was at least a *presumed* loyalty, after everything I'd done for you." I glared at her, unable to conceal my disgust. "It shouldn't take a contract signed in blood to keep friends from stabbing you in the back."

"Friends?" Tasha smirked. "Really? That's what you think we are?"

"My mistake. I guess you apologize to everyone you double-cross with designer shoes."

"I told you, those are *not* an apology. And all you've done for me? Let's not pretend you did any of that out of the goodness of your dumb ol' heart. You were just placating your own guilt."

"Like you're doing now?"

"Nooo." Tasha pointed her fork at me before stabbing it through a slice of grapefruit. "I'm *thanking* you. You tracked me down and offered a helpful tip."

"The tip was to be spotted by the Guard so you could be recruited through official channels."

"That's not the tip I found helpful," she answered in a smug sing-song.

"Clearly." I diverted my attention down at the food again, resisting the urge to grill her for the real reason she'd called this meeting. Tasha was not the type to go out of her way to thank anyone, let alone someone she didn't even consider a friend. The boots were more likely a bribe. For *what* was the real question.

The answer would come as soon as she suspected I'd let down my guard. Shoveling food into my face seemed a sufficient tactic as any to accomplish that. The deviled crab omelets had been a good call on Tasha's part. I soothed the tangy burn of the red chilies and lemon sauce with the pomegranate mimosa and hummed my contentment.

"I'm curious," Tasha said casually, taking the bait—or rather, assuming I'd taken hers, "did the council send a crotchety old demon to serve the other souls tea, too?"

"Beats me," I lied. Maybe I wasn't the sharpest scythe in the armory, but she wouldn't be getting any more *helpful tips* out of me any time soon. "I didn't stick around long enough to find out," I explained at her skeptical scowl.

It was true enough. Hecate's old companion had been ready to chew the legs off a table at the prospect of a lampad orgy waiting for her at the goddess's grove back in Tartarus. After a cup of Meng's tea, with her full memories restored, I imagined she was no better off than a cat in heat.

At least, that's how it had sounded the last time Hades and Persephone invited Bub and me over for dinner. Hecate's Grove bordered their garden. Still, it was better than having Tantalus, the cannibal king, living in their pool house.

The soul for Jahannam hadn't required tea. Zaynab had risen fully regressed from the glowing lagoon on the northern Isle of Eternity—a little tidbit I hadn't shared with the council, though they were suspicious enough at the notion I'd found her that way, and free-floating in the sea to boot. They hadn't released any details to the public, so I'd kept my mouth shut, too. I was in no hurry to find myself on the cover of Limbo's Laundry. Been there, done that.

"I guess you found a place to rent in the city," I said, prying with as much grace as Tasha had. Her lips quirked into a dry grin.

"I found a decent apartment in downtown Pandemonium, but I won't be able to move in until the first of May. For now, I'm staying at the Forks Inn."

"The one on the east side between the Styx and Cocytus?"

"Why? You gonna drop by for a visit?"

"I met you here, didn't I?" I shrugged, only mildly disappointed I hadn't weaseled the finer details out of her.

I had enough friends in Hell who could check into it if I really cared to know. But that wasn't my angle. I wanted Tasha to give up the goods the same way I had. I wanted her to feel tricked. Betrayed.

It was petty. I knew that. And I didn't have it in me to actually use the information to hurt her in any significant way. I just wanted her to know that I could. That she wasn't the only one with teeth and claws.

"Speaking of meetings…" Tasha's tone shifted, and I looked up. This was it. "I have an interview at the Hellagio next week."

"Wow." I gaped at her. "I mean, I figured your traitor-of-the-century prize money wouldn't last long, but I didn't think you'd have to resort to cocktail waitress gigs this soon."

Tasha ignored the ribbing and finished off her mimosa. "First of all, I'm applying for a dealer position. And this is just a steppingstone. A sexy, high-heeled boot in the door, if you will."

"The door to what, exactly? And why are you telling me?" I snapped, my patience finally reaching its breaking point.

"I thought you might put in a good word with the owner, since he's pals with your demonic beau." She blinked innocently, her lips pressing together as if it were taking all her strength not to add a resounding *duh* to the end of the request.

"Just because Asmodeus owns the Hellagio doesn't mean he has anything to do with interviewing staff." I shook my head. "Besides, he's on the Hell Committee. Their dealings with you have upset the council enough."

"Which is precisely why I think he'll be interested to know about my upcoming interview." Tasha crossed her legs, playfully dangling one of her sinful new boots. "I think I'd like to kick this exile experience up a notch, and I know a thing or two about seducing demons."

"Tack was a hellfire addict living in the slums of Limbo City," I said, biting back the observation that he hadn't required seduction so much as the promise of drugs. "Asmodeus is a prince of Hell. One of these things is not like the other."

Tasha bristled at my mention of Tack, but she didn't come to his defense as she had in the past. "If a slouch like you can entice Beelzebub, I'll take my chances." Her stony gaze bore into mine. "I just need you to make sure Asmodeus knows about the interview."

"And why should I? It's not like you and I are friends," I reminded her.

"But we're something, aren't we, precious?" She cocked her head. "You brought me supplies on the mortal side, and I haven't told a soul—or otherwise. I hate to imagine what anyone of importance might make of such a revelation."

"You wouldn't," I hissed, my poker face cracking without warning. Tasha's dimples twitched. The tick highlighted her satisfaction. She was winning this twisted little game, and she knew it. I sucked in a sharp breath and tried to regain my composure, though the fire in my blood was having none of it. "Good luck proving it," I added in a calm if quivering voice.

"How much evidence do you think the council would require?" Tasha whispered as she leaned closer. "I sure hope you have that fancy skeleton coin of yours in a good hiding place."

I swallowed the insult bubbling in my throat and instead knocked over my mimosa, sending the sticky juice in a straight line across the tabletop where it dripped off the edge and into Tasha's lap. She swore and snatched a napkin, attempting to save her miniskirt from further damage.

"Welp, it's been a blast catching up." I snagged another piece of bacon and stood, shoving it into my mouth before grabbing my old boots abandoned under the table. "I'll let Asmodeus know about your little interview."

"I knew you'd come to your senses." Tasha gave me a smug grin, managing to savor her victory even with a wet crotch.

"I doubt he'll show," I said. "And even if he does, you're not really his type."

"You think Jenni Fang is the only one who can pull off cool, militant indifference with panache?" Tasha's smile widened. "You haven't met every version of me yet, precious."

Asmodeus had been courting Jenni Fang for years, but she never had time for him or anyone else. Tasha had been present for the early days of his pining, which

I supposed was a factor in her scheme. There were plenty of rich demons in Hell, but only one involved with the reaper who had been willing to sacrifice Tasha to the council.

Maybe Tasha and I weren't friends, but whatever we were, I was glad it was enough to keep her attentions away from my demon. Not that she was Bub's type either, but I really didn't want the headache and paperwork that was sure to rain from the heavens if I had to put the vixen out of her misery for crossing that line.

I licked my fingers clean and fished a coin out of my pocket. "I'm keeping the boots," I said in lieu of a proper farewell. "I'd say you owe me *at least* that much."

Tasha snorted. "Whatever helps you sleep at night."

I rolled my coin and left her gloating face and the remnants of brunch behind. Along with my dignity.

CHAPTER TWO

*"We are not human beings having a spiritual experience;
we are spiritual beings having a human experience."*
—Pierre Teilhard de Chardin

WHILE TASHA'S BACKSTABBING had cost me a hefty payout from the Hell Committee, I did receive a nice bonus from Khadija's camp for delivering Zaynab. Not that I'd found a spare second to spend any of it. This was my first day off in over two months.

As captain of the newly reinstated Special Ops Unit, there was more pressure to perform. Though, so far, we'd only been tasked with helping Arden and the Posy Unit catch up on their massive backlog. Since I was also expected to continue identifying original believers, more and more high-risk souls were finding their way onto my list, too

The final moments that had once been a rare, morbid treat had become a never-ending game of hurry up and wait. Heart attacks were nowhere near as entertaining as killer clowns, but my apprentices were good sports about the new arrangement. I supposed the fatter paychecks helped.

Kevin and Eliza had saved enough coin for a romantic getaway in the faerie glades of Summerland. We were all taking a much-needed breather this weekend. It was just a shame that mine had kicked off with Tasha's blackmail brunch.

After leaving Pandemonium, I dropped by the harbor in Limbo City and changed back into my old boots in my private cabin on the ship. The skeleton coin Tasha had mentioned was stashed in a hidden compartment in the heel of my left boot. Not that I expected I'd have to use it anytime soon, but one could never be too careful. Besides, I wasn't up for breaking in a new pair of shoes today. Not with the evening I had ahead of me.

Bub and I were going to a party tonight. In Duat.

Okay, *party* was an understatement. Navigium Isidis was a major festival celebrating Isis and her past influence over the Mediterranean Sea. The ancient holiday was technically a Roman invention, introduced in Egypt during the reign of the Ptolemaic dynasty, but it had survived into the sixth century on the mortal side. After which, it became an exclusive event in Duat.

Not just anyone could celebrate with the old gods and their most venerated believers. So, naturally, I was suspicious when an invitation from Isis landed in my mailbox.

Just because the council hadn't outed me to the public, didn't mean word about my lingering *talent* wasn't circulating among the subcommittees. The under-the-table bribes to give certain souls priority had been proof enough of that. I assumed anything out of the ordinary was similarly linked to the revelation.

My first instinct was to politely refuse Isis's invite. I didn't have a great track record with Egyptian deities, and I still walked the other way any time I spotted Horus. But now that the Egyptian afterlife had merged with Summerland, they seemed more laid back and less calculating. Though they fiercely clung to their ceremonies and festivals, even the Hellenized ones.

Like many other deities of the ancient world, the major players of the Egyptian faith had been adopted by the neopagans. Their modern holidays were rooted in Celtic tradition, but they'd invited all the old gods to the party, no matter their origin. Like the Catholics and their saints, there were different favorites from coven to coven.

Isis was among the popular goddesses *de jour*. She was no stranger to foreign temples and pantheons. Still, Eternity-side, she preferred Egyptian traditions to the modern melting pot influence that many of the old gods had leaned into.

Zeus, on the other hand, hosted lavish parties on Mt. Olympus for all the neopagan holidays. He didn't hold as much clout with the mortals these days, but many of his children were altar staples. Especially Athena, who resented the inconvenience of having to leave her boutique in Limbo City to appease the souls of Summerland.

Of course, now that Athena was on the Afterlife Council, she had even less time for her business. She'd been forced to make Artemis a partner, merging the huntress goddess's line of leather capes, beaded quivers, and woodland apparel in with the ballgowns and clubwear.

The enchanted dummies that modeled the merchandise had to be upgraded with archery safety protocols after one shot a customer in the ass with an arrow. I hadn't been back to the shop since the news hit the cover of Limbo Weekly, but I needed a dress for tonight that didn't look as if it had been forged in hellfire and made for sinning. So, I was taking my chances.

As I descended the ramp from my ship to the dock, a cold wind pressed down on me, tearing my attention up at a dark silhouette in the sky. The wings were too large to belong to a nephilim, but Gabriel was off on some pilgrimage with Peter in the Jerusalem Mountains along the outskirts of Heaven. I didn't expect him back for at least another week.

"Great," I grumbled and shielded my eyes with one hand as Maalik dropped onto the pier, black robe billowing at his ankles. His wings folded sharply against his back, matching his sanctimonious scowl.

"You're being careless," he accused without greeting or context.

"And you're being a pain in my ass," I countered. "But what's new?"

Maalik grunted at the insult, but he fell in step beside me as I stalked off down the pier. "You were seen with Tasha Henry in Pandemonium this morning," he said under his breath. His gaze swept the harbor, taking in the scattered storks and dockworkers.

"That was fast." I shot him a sideways glare. "Are you spying on me, Councilor?"

"Don't be ridiculous." His cheeks flushed, though admitting something was absurd wasn't the same thing as denying it. "The Hell Committee is keeping a close eye on Ms. Henry. They've agreed to report her to the Afterlife Council the second she steps out of their territory."

"She's in no hurry to do that," I said, sparing him another scornful glance. "She only wanted to apologize for the trouble she's caused me. I didn't see the harm in meeting with her, and I wasn't aware of any law on the books forbidding it."

"You know there isn't." He fluttered a few steps ahead to cut off my path, forcing me to stop. "It will still look bad for you when the council finds out."

"What can they do?" I snapped, though my head was already filling with a million miserable answers. "They need me—and not just to track down more original believers. The soul market is swamped."

"That's true enough, but you should be careful regardless. Drawing the council's attention has never worked out well for you. I thought you'd appreciate the warning."

"I do." I sighed and gritted my teeth.

Maalik and I would never be friends, but there was a bridge between us that I didn't have it in me to burn. I couldn't imagine that he still carried a torch for me after all these years, which could only mean his kindness was meant to chisel away at his lingering guilt. New shoes were nice, but sound advice regarding the council was nothing to sneeze at.

"Thank you," I said, awkwardly biting off the words.

"You're welcome." Maalik dipped his chin in a stiff nod. Then his wings spread wide, stirring up another brisk wind as he darted back into the sky.

I had to assume he didn't know about my invitation to Isis's party. It wasn't like Maalik to pass up any opportunity to patronize, however well intentioned. Of course, I already knew what he'd have to say about me attending a high-profile event at which reapers were not typically welcome.

It wasn't that I *wanted* to go. Cordelia had convinced me.

The leader of the Woke Souls on the Isles of Eternity was adamant that I was a deity. That I deserved to walk among the gods, however new my spiritual transformation.

I couldn't even wrap my mind around the idea of laying claim to the islands off the coast of Limbo City where half the landmarks were named after me. Which was probably for the best, considering the council had shot down Cordelia's initial motion to name me as the territory's official deity. She wanted to try again—after building a stronger platform.

Unfortunately, this platform required a little participation on my part.

I knew squat about politics, and even less about being a goddess. I'd enjoyed a decade of relative peace by not rocking the boat, and I wasn't about to upset things for a fancy title I didn't want or need. The Woke Souls were the ones who wanted legitimacy. And as their involuntary liberator, they had certain… expectations of me.

I wouldn't start a war to force Eternity to recognize me as the islands' patron goddess, but refusing comradery from other deities who could help the cause would be seen as a slap in the face to the souls who revered me. Cordelia had said as much in her tearful plea that I accept the invitation and go as a representative of the Isles of Eternity. My island nation.

My island nation.

There was no way I could say that to Isis or any of the other gods without feeling like a total hack. But I'd let Cordelia guilt me into filling out the RSVP card, and now there was no backing out. The best I could hope for was to go unnoticed by anyone important and get the hell out of there before an opportunity to shove my foot in my mouth presented itself.

The first step of that plan involved a proper dress. I needed something that would blend in. Though it had to be flashy enough that I'd look like goddess material if someone snapped a picture and it ended up in the news. Cordelia's occasional visits to Limbo City for council meetings took her past plenty of newsstands.

With visions of fashion faux paus and rogue mannequin arrows flitting through my mind, I headed for the dock entrance. The lunch rush hadn't begun yet, so the travel booth on Market Street was empty. I plunked a coin in and selected the destination closest to Athena's Boutique.

If I were very lucky, Arachne would be on duty, and the goddesses would be out. Navigating deities was tiresome, and I was sure to have my fill of it tonight.

CHAPTER THREE

"Whatever our souls are made of, his and mine are the same."
—Emily Brontë

WHITE WAS NOT MY COLOR. I'd brushed off Arachne's rude assessment at the store, chalking it up to her black-on-black goth tendencies, but she wasn't lying. My wardrobe consisted primarily of dark leathers and denims, punctuated by pops of bold hues. Honestly, I was too pale to pull off a lighter palette. But since all the ladies in Duat would be wearing white, it was my best shot at going unnoticed.

"Hell have mercy."

Okay. Maybe not *entirely* unnoticed.

Bub made an appreciative noise low in his throat as he appeared behind me in the reflection of the full-length mirror in our bedroom. His hands settled on either side of my waist over the thick gold belt I'd picked up from a vendor at the harbor market. The buckle was decorated with a fat ruby and emerald scarab. It was a cheesy costume piece, but it worked for the theme of the night.

Bub's fingers ventured south, sliding over my hips until they reached the high thigh slits in my gown. A ripple of anticipation warmed my skin.

"We can't be late," I insisted, reading his mind as his eyes drank me in. "I don't want to draw attention."

"Darling, you'd have to arrive in a sealed box. It's the curse of being stunning, I'm afraid." He tilted his chin, admiring his freshly shaven face.

"Are we still talking about me?" I smirked and twisted my head to drop a kiss on his smooth throat. The beard had been fun, but this look was considerably more kissable.

Bub ignored my teasing and took a step back, letting his hands drop away so he could straighten the cuffs of his dusty blue suit jacket. "We look fit to crash a wedding, don't we?"

"They could stick us on top of the cake." My stomach grumbled at the thought of icing. I'd been too nervous to eat dinner, but there was sure to be celebratory sweets at the party. Maybe I'd finally relax once we got there and be able to enjoy a snack. If nothing else, there were plenty of goodies left in the latest basket Hecate had dropped off.

I was still getting used to calling the goddess of ghosts and crossroads my friend. After we'd collected an original believer for Tartarus, I had assumed she'd slink back to her secluded corner of the underworld and forget I existed. In a million years, I never would have anticipated her showing up on my front porch bearing gifts. After an awkward hour of small talk and stuffing our faces with wine and cheese, I hadn't expected her to return the following week for more, let alone every week since.

The small talk was becoming less uncomfortable. We were a work in progress, though I often wondered if her visits had more to do with taking a break from her amorous new guest than nurturing friendship.

Thinking of friendly goddesses and ulterior motives, I wondered what Isis had in store for me. It was too much to hope this was simply an effort to diversify Duat's ceremonies. They were quickly adapting as a new province of Summerland, but that integration concerned souls, not reapers.

What did she stand to gain by inviting me? I hated not knowing, and in my experience, surprises from the gods were rarely the nice kind.

I readjusted the golden bangles on my wrists and checked the laces on my sandals. The small clutch that matched my belt had enough room for a tube of lipstick, a spare coin, and a can of angelica mace. But something was missing. I was sure of it.

Or maybe that was just my hunger and anxiety conspiring with my better judgment.

"Are you ready, my lover goddess?" Bub turned toward the bedroom door, then did a double take at my wide-eyed expression in the mirror.

"You shouldn't call me that. Especially not in public."

"Darling, all of Eternity is aware we're lovers."

I grabbed my hips with both hands. "You know that's not the word I'm protesting."

Bub crossed the room to stand behind me again. "You've always been a goddess to me."

"But it's becoming too literal. The council might take it as a challenge to their authority. I'm not ready for that. I don't know if I'll ever be ready."

"You saved Eternity from absolute ruin—and on more than one occasion," Bub reminded me. His hands cupped my shoulders, gently squeezing. "Just because the pompous twats on the council don't want to admit it, doesn't make it any less true. You *are* a goddess, with or without any formal declaration from on high."

"I don't need their recognition." My cheeks flushed as the idea. As if I were a child waiting for a pat on the head. "This isn't about me—"

"I know, I know." Bub rolled his eyes. "Your pet souls want validity."

"Oh god, don't call them that." I cringed and shot him a dirty look.

"Well, what would you prefer I call them? They are yours to name as you choose, after all. Lanians? Lananites? Lanatics?"

"Please, stop." I groaned and covered my face with both hands. "They already have a name. Woke Souls. Let's leave well enough alone, shall we?"

Bub snorted. "We're going to have to work on that modesty of yours. Humble is not a trait meant for goddesses."

"Says who? That could be my claim to fame. Lana Harvey, goddess of confusion and humility, who occasionally parties with the faithless."

"*Formerly* faithless," he corrected. "They certainly believe in something—or rather, *someone*—now, don't they?"

"But why?" I pouted. "Even if the council does recognize me as their official deity, I no longer control the throne's power. There's no better or worse place I can send them for good or bad deeds. The isles are theirs to do with as they please. They don't *need* me. There's nothing more I can do for them."

"Perhaps it's not about *doing* more."

"Then what?"

"Have you considered this may be a matter of maintenance?" Bub arched a brow. "You did save them from a miserable fate. They may fear your disinterest puts them at risk for being cast back into the sea if the council turns on them. A patron goddess would serve as another veil of protection."

"Like I stand a chance against the council." I scoffed.

"You've thwarted their plans before," Bub said. "You raised islands and woke sleeping souls. Are you really prepared to let some jealous, crusty old gods erase those accomplishments?"

It was a fair question, but I didn't have an answer.

Rolling over and playing dead was the smarter, easier option. Besides, it was hard to miss something if you never really considered it yours in the first place. Though, somewhere along the way, I supposed I *had* begun to consider the isles and the Woke Souls mine. And they certainly considered me theirs.

They'd even built me a home on the northern island, in the clearing surrounded by the Harvian Wood. I stayed there whenever I visited. Bub and I hadn't talked about it, but I was sure one of his winged spies had overheard Cordelia's invitation to live with them permanently. I'd told her that I would think about it. At the time, I had been high on the bliss of their company and a rejuvenating bath in the magical lagoon that was also my namesake.

Bub's warm breath caressed my neck. "Don't misunderstand, dearest. Of course I selfishly want you all to myself. But I'm a seasoned demon, and I know how these things unfold. I will always be here to stand by your side, as long as you allow it—"

I twisted around and touched a finger to his lips, ending the speech before it reduced me to tears. "I will always allow it." There was no doubt about that. I pulled my hand away and kissed him. Just a chaste brush of lips. Once, twice. If I covered him in lipstick, we'd be late for sure. "You know," I whispered against his mouth, "standing by my side is nice and all, but I'll allow a lot more than that when we get home tonight."

"Is that so?" Bub's lips curled into a small grin.

"Absolutely." I stole one last kiss then turned back to the mirror to resume my fretting over what I'd forgotten. "And the sooner we get there, the sooner we can leave," I said, forcing a polite smile at myself. I didn't buy the sincerity of it any more than I was sure Isis would.

But a promise was a promise. Cordelia would be crushed if I bailed now. She'd constructed a fantasy world in her mind, an Eternity where the veteran goddesses accepted me as one of their own and told me the secret ingredient for securing a proper myth and afterlife.

If such a thing existed, I was sure none of the goddesses had any intention of sharing the knowledge with me. Cordelia was right about one thing, though. Isis definitely wouldn't teach me the secret deity handshake if I insulted her by refusing to go to her fancy-pants party.

I was prepared to return without said handshake or secret sauce recipe. I was just hoping my attendance would at least buy enough good will with Cordelia and the Woke Souls that they'd allow me to bring Bub the next time I visited. It was a long shot, but they had to know there would be no permanent move for me without my demon consort. And although Bub was at the top of that wish list, my hellhounds, running water, and a proper dock pier were close behind.

But this was all theoretical. For now.

At the moment, my biggest concern was Isis's motive for inviting me to her party. Goddesses always had their reasons. This was going to cost me something. I just didn't know what yet.

"If you're not up for this, you don't have to go tonight," Bub said, squeezing my shoulders again.

I sighed and grabbed my clutch off the dresser. "Yeah, unfortunately, I do."

CHAPTER FOUR

*"At a formal dinner party, the person nearest death
should always be seated closest to the bathroom."*
—*George Carlin*

THIS WAS NOT MY FIRST glimpse beyond the gates of
Duat. When Grim had sent me after Khadija's replace-
ment, I'd been granted entry to the temple of Osiris to
witness the Weighing of the Hearts ceremony in the Hall
of Two Truths. For souls of their faith, it was a serious
rite of passage that determined whether they were pure
enough to pass into Aaru, the Egyptian paradise.

While there were plenty of dangers and lessons to be
learned on a soul's journey through Duat, the realm
wasn't exactly a hell region. It was classified as an underworld, but it functioned as a mostly neutral middle
ground, like Limbo City—just with less shopping and
more riddles.

The merger with Summerland hadn't changed much
at the gates or the seaports, but some construction had
taken place at the realms' northern border, near the Hapi

River that encircled Duat. The far western bend of the river marked the border of Aaru, which had remained an exclusive territory, but beyond the river's northern bank, where the desert faded into the Annwn Forest that marked Summerland's *former* southern border, a section of trees had been cleared.

This made way for an avenue that tied into the Valhalla Highway. The street ended in a roundabout set between a stretch of parking lots built in the shade of trees that had survived the infrastructure's birth. From there, it was a short walk down the bank to reach the footbridge built over the Hapi.

I was sure I'd oversold my interest in seeing the new developments, but Bub was a gentleman and didn't call out my cowardice. We coined off to Summerland's main gate and hailed a taxi to take us the rest of the way.

Arriving at Duat's seaport gate would have made for a showier entrance, but while I'd promised Cordelia I would go to the party, I'd made no commitment to organize a parade or prance about like a peacock.

I'd witnessed plenty of humans do the covert drop-in at funerals. They'd find a familiar face or two to vouch for them, sign the guestbook, and peace out. I doubted Isis had a guestbook for this shindig, but I was hoping I'd at least spot Ammit or Anubis before ransacking the buffet table and taking off.

The Valhalla Highway was hilly, and our faun taxi driver had a lead hoof. I would have liked to have blamed the flip-flop of my stomach on that rather than the sight of the first exit sign for Duat, but my heart rate climbed a little higher with each mile marker we passed.

Bub squeezed my thigh. "It's not too late to turn back," he whispered loud enough to be heard over the panpipe music crackling through the taxi speakers.

"We've made it this far." I gave him a weak smile and then looked out the window, watching for the stone archway that had been pictured in Limbo Weekly to announce the grand opening. That had been a few years ago, but this would be my first time seeing it in person.

The taxi slowed as our driver signaled and moved onto the off ramp. At the stop sign, he turned left onto Amun Way, following the direction of a billboard that featured pyramids and a sphinx with flashing LED lights for eyes. Thankfully, the cheesy tourist trappings ended there.

It was difficult to tell where the entrance to Duat was until we were practically on top of it. The stone arch crested below the tree line, and it was recessed a ways inside the forest, marking some midpoint in the gently winding street. The design was simple and archaic. No toll booths or guards waited to check IDs or demand our reason for being there, but occasionally, a faint flicker caught my attention from the trees. There were no doubt cameras to document the comings and goings of so many new faces.

When we reached the roundabout on the other side of the forest, our driver took the first exit and moved into a long drop-off line. More vehicles were quickly filling the parking lots.

The Congress of the Sphinx had resisted joining the Summerland Society for so long, but there was no denying the union had bolstered their economy. Pagans with Egyptian leanings flocked to the formerly purist territory. Festivals that had once been the size of a backyard pool party now rivaled Mardi Gras. It was this surplus of mixed-bag pagans that I intended to use as camouflage to get in and out on the down-low.

"Probably best if we settle up now," our faun driver said. "Lots of fares in Olympus and Elysium waiting for a ride." His nose twitched as he shot a nervous glance in his rearview mirror. I doubted he taxied many demons or reapers through Summerland. I hoped the souls were less observant.

Bub tossed the driver a coin and opened his door, offering me his hand after he exited the car. Soon enough, we were swept up in the heap of souls spilling down the bank toward the river. They were less skittish here than in Limbo City, where one could bump into a god or a devil on any given street corner. But we were in soul country now.

In these parts, the gods dressed for distinction and praise. It was easy to assume anyone without a golden headdress or flock of attendants carrying them around in a palanquin was just another soul. I wasn't used to being jostled about so carelessly, but I didn't complain. This had been my plan, and so far, it was working.

Bub swore as an elbow grazed his shoulder. The culprit mumbled an apology before scampering off to catch up with his party. A closer look would have easily revealed our soulless nature, but all eyes were on the festive scene unfolding beyond the river.

The Hapi flowed bright and clear beneath the new bridge. On the opposite side, a garden waited, ripe with peach and pomegranate trees, jasmine and rose bushes. Children played with sistra and bells, doing their best to keep rhythm with the drums that echoed from a Greco-Roman pavilion in the distance. The open-air columns surrounded a massive statue of Isis, though in her more traditional fashion, with kohl-lined eyes and gilded wings.

Bub squeezed my hand, drawing my attention to the pair of white-robed souls passing out flower crowns to guests as they crossed the bridge. Just what my good hair day needed. I made a face, earning another hand squeeze from my demon.

"Those are priestesses," he whispered. "They serve the gods here, and they may very well have been ordered to report your arrival. If you want to avoid detection, accept the flowers and don't make eye contact."

I pressed my lips together as he tugged me toward the robed woman on his side of the bridge. At this angle, I could use his body as a shield. Another good idea to limit my exposure. Of course, it might have gone smoother if I hadn't brought the iconic Prince of Demons as my plus-one.

"Your Highness." The priestess dipped her chin in a polite nod then stole a glance over his shoulder at me. Her breath hitched, but she didn't say anything more as she adorned us with crowns of white roses.

I mumbled my thanks, and we moved back into the fray of souls. It wasn't until we reached the grassy lawn on the opposite side of the river that I realized all the other guests were wearing crowns of daisies and carnations.

"Shit. Shit. Shit," I chanted, taking in the crowd. If we hadn't stood out before, we certainly did now.

"Should we find another couple to trade with?" Bub suggested, immediately recognizing the problem.

"Too late," I said through clenched teeth as the sea of guests parted for an entourage wearing familiar golden falcon masks. At their center was a broad-chested schmuck wearing a larger, more ornate falcon headdress.

"You came!" Horus shouted. He shook his clasped hands at us in a showy gesture of gratitude.

"Yeah… Hi." I spared him an awkward wave. Insulting a god in the presence of his followers wasn't a good look for anyone—and it was likely illegal in Duat. The neutral liberties of Limbo City did not apply here.

"Isis will be so pleased." Horus's smile seemed genuine, but with our sordid past, I wasn't about to let my guard down. "Come!" He waved an arm toward the pavilion on the hill. "I'll take you to her."

"No thanks—" I grunted as Bub poked me in the ribs. His eyes darted to the side, drawing my attention to a soul livestreaming the scene with a cell phone. We were about to be GraveSpace famous. Super. My attention snapped back to Horus. "I mean… I'm sure Isis is busy with all the festivities. I'd hate to interrupt."

That seemed the most dignified way to decline if I was being recorded. *Oh darn, I left the stove on,* was just too blatantly spineless.

"It's quite all right," Horus insisted. "The main event won't start for a while yet, and she wants to greet you personally."

"Oh…" I stared at him, waiting for another respectable excuse to come to me. But none did. "Okay then."

Horus's smile sharpened in the corners of his mouth, a tribute to the double-sided sword of our past alliance. "Onward!" he cheered, radiating with more mirth than any cutthroat god had a right to.

The falcon-headed attendees widened their circle, enclosing Bub and me along with Horus as we began the climb up the hill. The transition from guest to potential prisoner had been unexpected, and I struggled to process my mounting panic. Every sound was too sharp. Every watchful eye seemed tinged with malice. The echo of the drums grew louder until I could feel it infringing on the thrum of my pulse, trembling in my neck and temples, rattling my lungs.

My hand in Bub's was suddenly slick. I was sure the nerves weren't mine alone, but at least he could burst into a swarm of flies if he sensed danger. I'd have a slightly harder time fleeing, though I was sure my demon's foot soldiers would do their best to carry me to safety. That's not to say we'd make it very far with the giant falcon at Horus's command chasing after us.

Now *there* was a way to go viral on GraveSpace.

A herd of giggling children ran circles around the columns of the pavilion. They clutched toy sailboats in their hands and danced them along an invisible river as they declared which god or goddess they ferried through the afterlife. When they saw the golden falcon heads, they squealed and paused their play to bow as Horus passed. Their curious faces squinted up at Bub and me, no doubt wondering who we were and why we walked among their sacred pantheon.

Horus directed us past the sheltered statue of Isis and the drummers seated at her feet. The opposite side of the hill was less hectic, unrolling into a grassy meadow bordered by the Hapi. The river curled inland, outlining the western corner of Isis's estate, before twisting north again toward Duat's border.

Near the center of the meadow stood a temple. The architecture was more distinctly Egyptian, as were the immaculate hieroglyphs and bas-reliefs covering the temple walls. This was a new structure, probably intended to appease the wave of fresh tourists.

Like the statue in the pavilion, it ignored the Roman influence of the later kingdoms, an agenda Osiris had pushed during his term on the Afterlife Council in the eighteen hundreds. His request for a grant to restore Duat to its original ancient glory had been denied despite a resurgence of interest in Egyptian mythology after Napoleon's invasion and the discovery of the Rosetta Stone.

To be fair, the attention was more historic and scientific in nature than religious. That's not to say it didn't inspire a few new secret societies and cults, but the neopagan movement that spawned a devout subculture didn't happen for another century. I suspected the merger with Summerland had come with the promise of allocated funds that were finally bringing Osiris's vision to life.

It wasn't until we reached the bottom of the hill that I fully appreciated the massive scale of the temple. The sandstone walls, baked golden by the sun, stood at least five stories tall. A bust of Isis in her sky goddess form marked the entrance of the temple. Two pillars engraved with hieroglyphs supported her spread wings, welcoming guests into the courtyard beyond.

"Lovely, isn't it?" Horus called over his shoulder as we wove through the hissing grass. "There's still a bit of construction going on inside, but it should be ready in time for the grand opening this summer to celebrate Isis's birthday."

"Wonderful," Bub replied, filling the void of my petrified silence before it could be mistaken for rudeness. "If it looks anything like the outside, I'm sure it's magnificent."

"Unfortunately, you'll have to wait until then to see it." Horus paused near the pillars holding his winged mother's likeness aloft and offered Bub an apologetic smile. "Isis wishes to speak with Lana in private."

I couldn't tell if Horus's guards only *seemed* closer because we'd come to a stop, or if they sensed my fight-or-flight instincts kicking in. I shot the one nearest to me a dirty look and then turned back to the god of offers I couldn't refuse.

"Well, aren't I special?" At least on this side of the hill there were no nosy souls with cell phones. Maybe it wasn't too late to give the stove excuse a go.

"Don't worry, love." Bub leaned down to kiss my cheek, and I felt the tickle of a tiny wing behind my ear. "I'll be right *here*, waiting for you."

CHAPTER FIVE

*"Many of us crucify ourselves between two thieves —
regret for the past and fear of the future."*
—*Fulton Ourser*

CALL ME PARANOID, but I half expected guards to jump out of the shadows the second I stepped foot inside Isis's fancy new temple. She'd never threatened me, per se. But I supposed I'd given her plenty of reason to despise me, however unintentional the consequences of my actions had been.

The laundry list of slights dated back nearly a century, beginning with Ruth Summerdale, a soul whose mother had sloppily initiated her into a cult of Isis in her youth. The Congress of the Sphinx made a grab for souls they had any shred of claim to, no matter how ignorant the soul in question was regarding Egyptian traditions and rituals.

Ruth wouldn't have lasted twenty seconds in Duat. I didn't regret enlisting Gabriel's help to score her a contract at the Three Fates Factory. Back then, soul transfer violations had been a way of life for me. I kept a cleaner record these days, especially now that I was responsible for more high-risk harvests.

The sanctuary inside Isis's temple was lined with scaffolding. Along the far side of the room, it boxed in a trio of large, half-finished statues being carved into the sandstone. The other three walls were covered in hiero-glyphs, cartouches, and illustrations detailing the mysterious rites of Isis's cult and the goddess's role in the Osiris myth. The paint glistened, still wet in some places, and faint etchings in the stone revealed a glimpse of scenes to come.

"This is a pleasant surprise," a melodic voice greeted me.

I turned to watch Isis enter the room. The hem of her white gown glittered with gold that hissed as it brushed over the stone floor. More gold dripped from her sleeves, outlining the feathers of her faux wings. A cow-horn headdress rose from her nest of black braids, and I had a sudden vision of being gored to death.

"I must confess, I wasn't expecting you to show," Isis said.

"Oh, really? Well…" I hiked a thumb at the temple entrance behind me. "I can come back another time, if you're busy."

I'd been around long enough not to get swept up in a goddess's maternal, salt-of-the-earth edition. Many of them were dual-natured. Others, like Isis, had taken it a step further. The facets of their personalities were so extreme that, in their prime, they'd birthed new deities like a dandelion gave off seeds, spreading their faith to distant lands. Though the Treaty of Eternity had put an end to divine propagation, the old gods retained the benevolent and vengeful traits that had once inspired empires to rise and fall.

"I'm *glad* you're here." Isis grinned at my obvious distress. "It's time you and I had a heart-to-heart."

"Is it? Are you sure? I mean, there's no rush. And you have so many guests out there waiting to see you—" I shot another nervous glance at the entrance.

Isis sucked in a slow breath, causing her enormous horns to sway. One way or another, I just knew I was going to find myself on the wrong end of them.

"I realize our shadow dealings have not always been to your liking," she said, folding her hands. "Horus is efficient, though his methods can be abrasive."

"Abrasive?" I snorted, unable to help myself. "Is that what we're calling it now when someone blackmails another into breaking the law?"

Isis hitched a dark brow. "Would you rather he have reported you to the council for murdering a deity?"

My mouth went dry. "I don't know what you're talking about."

That was my story, and I was sticking to it. Besides, Wosyet had been working for Seth and the rebels. And I'd axed her—quite *literally*—in self-defense. Not that it would matter to the council, which was why I was fully prepared to lie my ass off.

Horus had sworn to keep my secret in exchange for tracking down candidates to replace Winston on the Throne of Eternity. It had all gone horribly wrong in the end, but I'd upheld my end of the deal. Which was more than I could say for his blabber-beak.

"Your actions were justified." Isis held up her hands, acknowledging my bristled offense. "But then, so were Horus's. Though Tutankhamun was not suited for the throne, Grim would have let it destroy him and Eternity, too. He was blinded by his ambition."

King Tut. That had been Winston once upon a time, but even after Meng's regression tea, all I'd been able to see was the dying boy I'd found in a hospital bed, who had accepted his death and duty to Eternity with all the grace of Mother Teresa.

"Winston definitely needed to be replaced," I agreed. "But Horus went about it the wrong way. The threats were unnecessary."

"He offered money and political allegiance first," Isis was quick to remind me. "And then he negotiated your salvation by abdicating his seat on the council and merging our territory with Summerland—even after the part you played in the eternal death of Tutankhamun." A hint of bitterness slipped into her tone, but I wasn't ready to cower yet.

"If by political allegiance you mean his overzealousness in having me promoted, that was a selfish means to put me in contact with more souls for his illegal side job."

"So you *didn't* enjoy the juicier paychecks?"

"Oh sure," I admitted. "I also loved the big red target on my back that drew the attention of politicians and rebels alike who thought they could use me to get to Grim or the throne. That was a blast."

Isis gritted her teeth, and for a second, I worried I'd said too much. I hadn't come here to compare sins and scars. I'd just wanted to do a quick pop-in to appease my half-baked wannabe cult. But it sure felt as if she were trying to weasel a thank you out of me for all the hell Horus had put me through at her behest, and that so wasn't happening.

Not today. Not ever.

The bigger dilemma taking shape in the back of my mind was *why* she wanted the thanks. Why she seemed to *need* it. And why now? Years after the fact.

There was a favor waiting to be asked. And if the past were any indication, likely a threat waiting to be made, too—if I didn't immediately accept her proposal. Maybe she planned to skip the coin this time and barter with guilt and gratitude. Had they blown through the budget so soon with these latest additions?

"Look…" Isis folded her hands again, regaining her composure. "It is no secret that you were cast in a different mold than your kindred reapers. And it's no secret, at least among the council and subcommittees, that you have maintained some of the abilities with which Khadija gifted you. There are those who view this as a threat. I, however, see it as an opportunity to forge an alliance."

"An alliance?" I scoffed. "Will this alliance require me to do something illegal on your behalf?"

Isis shook her head, drawing my attention to her horns again. "Nothing illegal, but it *is* of utmost importance. And you would be properly compensated."

"You might have led with that." I folded my arms and tried not to scowl at her. "I guess it couldn't hurt to hear you out." Though as soon as the words left my mouth, I wondered how true they were.

"Thank you." Isis bobbed her chin in an appreciative nod, and I took a step back as her horns tilted in my direction.

I realized my error instantly. It was rude to insinuate a goddess as practiced as she might accidentally maim a guest. My face flushed with embarrassment, but I let my gaze rotate around the room, feigning interest in the murals.

"Our myths are fascinating, aren't they?" Isis said, taking my attention to heart. She waved one of her gilded sleeves at a finished illustration depicting her search for the pieces of Osiris after he'd been dismembered. "So many have been lost to time and ruin, but these few sacred stories persist. They remind us of the most valuable lessons we've learned."

"Like, just because it fits, you shouldn't always sits?" I asked as my gaze snagged on another image, this one of Osiris locked inside the custom box Seth had used to trap him. Though, I didn't see the sinister god of the desert and disorder. He was nowhere to be found on any of the walls, despite his roles in the pictured myths.

"I'm a forgiving sister—to a point," Isis said, accurately predicting for whom I searched. "I made the mistake of taking pity on my brother once before. But I will not enable his return this time."

"I don't think you have to worry about that. I heard Grim left him in as many pieces as you found your husband. Poetic justice, I suppose."

"That or he was hoping to frame someone from my faith," Isis suggested. "Regardless, death alone cannot defeat the divine—not while they are revered on the mortal side, anyway."

"And Seth is?" I made a face.

"Everyone has someone." Isis motioned for me to follow her. The hiss of her gown echoed in the temple, shifting in tone as we turned down a long corridor and stepped inside a smaller sanctuary with more wall art. "Our cults have shrunk into obscurity, but a few factions remain, altered as they may be."

"Well, I certainly haven't harvested any of Seth's mortal followers." The idea made my skin crawl. Dealing with his Eternity-side supporters had been tedious enough. "I thought the Treaty of Eternity put an end to spontaneous resurrections," I added.

"Who said anything about spontaneous?" Isis tilted her gaze up at a new painting. This one featured a proud Egyptian queen at a banquet table. A Roman emperor sat at the opposite end, his smug grin hidden behind a wine chalice.

"Cleopatra and Mark Antony?" I guessed out loud, not knowing how to read the cartouches bookending the mural.

Isis nodded. "I'm told you nearly harvested Odin some winters past."

"Yup." I cringed at the reminder. That had been the first soul Tasha had tried to poach from me. Some lessons are harder to learn than others, I guessed. I'd also lost my coin, and Gabriel and I had ended up walking for miles across the snowy Alaskan tundra to find it so we could make our way back home.

"An unfortunate twist of fate," Isis said. "Or rather, an *error* of the Fates. It happened less often when the gods were allowed to reveal themselves in their fleshly incarnations." Her attention shifted to the man in the mural. "They called him Dionysus born anew, but Serapis borrowed traits from several gods of various pantheons. Like a divine Frankenstein's monster with the face of an angel. I don't think he ever felt he belonged anywhere. Except with me."

The painting made sense now. It wasn't some random piece of ancient Egyptian history. It was *her* history.

"You were really Cleopatra?" I asked. "That wasn't just a pretentious queen looking for clout?"

Isis smirked. "I've been a great many mortal queens. But she was my last. When Serapis allowed the humans to call him Dionysus, he angered Apollo's royal meat puppet in Rome. From there, our days were numbered. Do you see my pearls?" She pointed at the large orbs hanging from her ears. "They were holy relics of my most sacred cult, talismans meant to choose and bless my next incarnation."

"Where are they now?" I asked, wondering if tomb raiders had gotten to them before Napoleon went on his looting spree through Egypt.

"Well…" Isis gave me a sheepish smile. "I ate one." At my bewildered stare, she added, "It was to prove a point." As if that somehow made it any less absurd.

"And the other?"

"Everything happened so fast when Apollo's forces took over."

"You mean Octavian's forces?" I asked, earning a withering stare from Isis. *Royal meat puppet.* Of course. Go big or go home.

"The remaining pearl was with me when I learned Serapis had departed," Isis continued, her expression growing soft and distant. "That's when I abandoned Cleopatra's fleshly form."

"So Apollo stole it?"

"For a time. He took it to Rome and split it in half to adorn the ears of Venus in the Pantheon. There it stayed for over a hundred years, until my cult reclaimed it and burned the temple to the ground."

"If they had the pearl, why didn't your cult bring you back to the mortal side?"

"They tried. You can knock on a door all you like, but unless someone answers, there is no meeting of minds or spirits."

"And you weren't interested in going?"

"Not without Serapis. I never did find him when I emerged in my divine form in Eternity. He had many enemies. Many gods who felt he'd infringed on their personas and patrons."

"Did Osiris feel that way?" It was a nosy question, but she was spilling plenty of tea all by herself. When in Rome—*er*, Duat.

"I'm sure. Serapis replaced him as my consort for a time." Isis sighed and ushered me toward the opposite wall and a new mural. This one was of another Ptolemaic power couple, possibly the first, considering the chiseled profile of Alexander the Great standing beside the pharaoh, one hand resting on his shoulder. "Our first union of the flesh, as Ptolemy and Berenice. Our affair included seven lifetimes of blood-soaked trysts scattered over three centuries, but it began and ended with this dynasty.

"Don't misunderstand. I love my husband. Our fates have been entwined since birth. But before the treaty that stabilized our myths on this side of the grave, we evolved at the whim of mortals. Fleshly embodiments were our only means of influencing the story, our only chance to have lives of our own making, however brief and fragile. Osiris took pleasure in seizing the reins of his fate from time to time, as well."

"You must miss it." I frowned at Isis, still grasping for the meaning of this rambling history lesson. My patience was waning.

As interesting as I was sure her many lives had been, I wasn't about to spend all night roaming her new temple, listening to her recount the years she'd spent among the mortals, simultaneously fulfilling and inventing her mythos. If there was a point, it was time to get to it.

"Is that what you want my help with—finding these magical pearl halves so you can play invasion of the body snatchers again?" I demanded.

Isis's head jerked around, bringing her horns dangerously close to my face again. But I didn't move this time. A few stitches seemed like an acceptable way to dodge the rest of this conversation.

"Not quite." A cold edge hardened her nostalgic story-time voice. "I *do* need help fetching the pearl halves, but only to keep them safe. My cult may have forged the talisman, but it can be used to birth any number of divine manifestations on the mortal side. I know where the halves are. I just need a reaper with psychopompic skills to facilitate the job."

"Why me?" I had to ask, especially if my special Khadija-given talents weren't required. "Sounds like any old reaper will do."

"Sounds like," Isis agreed with a plastic smile. "But Horus insisted that we offer the job to you first. With your pending goddess status, he assumed you'd be eager to prove yourself."

"Well, you know what happens when you assume. You end up with salty salad dressing." I broke her fuming stare and waved an arm at the painted walls. "I noticed you skipped that particular myth. Good call."

Of course she'd omitted it. That one had included Seth—eating lettuce Isis had doused with Horus's *ball*salmic dressing. Incest was far from the only ick factor among the ancient deities. I made a mental note to skip the salad bar on my way out of Duat.

"Well, at least I've kept my promise to my son." Isis opened an arm toward the exit. "Enjoy the party."

"Thanks for the tour," I said, my civility returning at the prospect of food and a swift departure. But despite my best efforts, a nagging question foiled my escape. I paused in the doorway and ran a hand down the smooth sandstone before looking over my shoulder. "Just out of professional curiosity, who else did you have in mind for this little treasure hunt?"

Isis shrugged. "We're hard-pressed to find an available reaper on such short notice, but I know of at least one who's actively looking for work." My shock was too sudden to mask, and the goddess's lips quirked into a satisfied grin. "I suppose she'd appreciate a divine alliance even more than you."

Damn. And I'd been so close to washing my hands of this mess.

CHAPTER SIX

*"The eternal quest of the individual human being
is to shatter his loneliness."*
—*Norman Cousins*

THERE WAS NO PARTY to be had after leaving Isis's temple. I needed somewhere private to fume over this new dilemma, a safe place to piss and moan. When Bub and I returned to the manor, I didn't even take the time to change my clothes before stalking out to the back patio.

It was dark. Here, only the stars could judge me. Well, the stars and the button-eyed octopus watching from the garden pond. Even Ursula could tell I was having a bad night. The murky water bubbled as she sank below the surface. It was a wonder the stars didn't blink out, my mood was so toxic.

The lanterns clicked on, and then Bub joined me with our butler hot on his heels.

"You're home early," Rupert said, wringing a dish towel between his hands. The skin around his horn puckered as he took in my sour expression. "Did you get enough to eat? Shall I fix a sharp cutlery board?" At our confused silence, he added, "With the smoked meats and cheeses… and tiny knives?"

"*Charcuterie* board," Bub corrected. "Please. And perhaps some wine to go with it." He waited for Rupert to duck back inside before cautiously approaching me as if I were a feral cat. "A little merlot puts everything in a rosier light."

"She's going to give the job to Tasha if I don't accept," I snarled. Not that I needed to tell him, seeing as how his buzzy backup had surely relayed my conversation with Isis by now.

Bub reached for me, but I twisted away and stormed off toward the far end of the patio. As soon as I reached the edge, I turned and cut a path for the opposite side. Maybe if I paced long enough, my feet would catch up with my runaway train of thought.

"Would that be the worst thing in the world?" Bub asked. "Even if they did give her immunity in Duat, it's not like you care for the realm."

"But it's part of Summerland now. They'll push for her freedom there, too. I just know it."

"Still, not the end of the world." Bub stepped into my path and caught my shoulders. He pressed a kiss to my forehead and wrapped his arms around my back, smothering me in his cinnamon-sweet warmth. "She'll never be welcome in Tartarus. Hecate will see to that."

The Greek underworld was sandwiched between Summerland and Hell, and accessible through the gates of both. It was an independent territory in its own right, but any members from the land who served on the Afterlife Council did so on behalf of the Summerland Society. Though, the length of Tasha's leash wasn't my only concern.

"What if it gets out that I was offered the job first?" I whispered. "Everyone will think I'm a coward—or worse, lazy. Cordelia and the Woke Souls will be so disappointed. Isis holds plenty of sway with the Summerland Society now. That's two votes on the council I'd be forfeiting—Athena's and the Green Man's."

"I thought you didn't care if they officially declared you a deity," Bub said. His fingers found the knots in my shoulders and neck, and he began working his magic on me, kneading endorphins free to combat the anxiety. I pressed my face into his chest and groaned.

"I can't believe Isis would trust someone like *Tasha*. What a dummy."

"The dumbest," Bub agreed, his hot breath curling around my ear.

"Maybe she's bluffing."

"Maybe," he echoed.

"But what if she isn't?"

"So what if she isn't?"

"Are you even listening to me?" I snapped.

"Of course I'm listening." Bub nuzzled my curls and moved his hands lower until they found my ass. "Your body may be divine, but it doesn't render my ears useless, love."

"I have to make a decision by morning. That's when Anubis plans to leave for Egypt—or Hell, to track down Tasha if I'm a no-show."

"But this weekend was supposed to be ours." Bub pouted. "If you need a fancy title, I'm still prepared to worship you as my lover goddess." His lips brushed my neck, and then a forked tongue painted a hot, wet line across my skin. I shuddered as my knees were almost rendered useless.

The sound of the back door derailed Bub's seduction, and the sight of Rupert's spread reminded me of the brunch with Tasha and the unpleasant news that I'd yet to share.

"Thank you. That will be all," Bub said as soon as Rupert set the patio table, his libido having no patience for the usual polite script. But before my demon could resume his wooing, a pack of wild dogs appeared from around the corner of the house, lured in by the smell of fresh treats. "Bloody hell," he hissed.

Kevin's helljacks were staying with us while he and Eliza were away. It was too much fluff and drool for one bed, especially a bed Bub and I had big plans for over the next few days, so all the pooches had been banished to the garage for the weekend—the garage with a doggy door so no one took a shit where they shouldn't.

"Didn't you feed these heathens?" Bub grumbled. Rupert froze in the open doorway, his stealthy retreat cut short.

"Of course, Master Beelzebub. Twice, in fact," he said. "Shall I offer them a third helping?"

"I think not," I answered before Bub could suggest stuffing the dogs silly.

Kevin would not be thrilled if he had to roll the hell-jacks out of here. And the hellhounds took up enough space in our bed as it was.

"We'll share our snacks." I nodded at Rupert, giving him permission to leave us. Then I wriggled free of Bub's embrace and went to the table to select a few morsels for our uninvited dinner guests.

Coreen was too cool to beg for treats. She nipped at her grown pups, trying to tame their excitement. Meanwhile, Saul sat at my feet, watching with rapt attention, slobber dripping from his jowls. When my hand hovered over the selection of cubed cheeses, he licked his nose.

I tossed each doggo two pieces each and then stuffed a handful of pretzels in my mouth and plucked a few grapes free of their stems. If I couldn't pace, stress eating would have to do.

My demon whimpered out a frustrated sigh and reached for the wine bottle. "I guess we always have tomorrow."

"Unless I end up in Egypt," I said, cramming an olive and a slice of prosciutto in after the grapes. "I've had about enough of Tasha's bullshit. I met with her in Pandemonium this morning," I finally confessed.

"You did what?" The wine bottle slipped in Bub's hands, and he clutched it to his chest at the last second, saving it from a tragic fate.

"Yeah," I mumbled past the mouthful of food. "She's applying for a job at the Hellagio, and she threatened to rat me out to the council for helping her get by on the mortal side if I didn't put in a good word with Asmodeus. Can you believe the nerve of that backstabbing twit?"

"Oh, I absolutely can," Bub said, eyes wide and unblinking. "What I can't believe is how gullible you are for meeting with her in the first place. Haven't you learned your lesson with that snake yet?"

"Gullible?" I shrieked. The effect was somewhat muted with my bulging cheeks that were suddenly on fire. I swallowed hard and tried again. "Gullible? It's not like I met with her to go shopping."

"Oh really? I suppose you picked up the new boots after?" Bub popped the cork free of the wine and took a long drink straight from the bottle.

"They were a gift—a bribe," I amended. "An apology," I revised again, not giving a damn how insistent Tasha had been that she wasn't sorry. She *would* be. I'd see to that.

"Mmhmm." Bub glared at me and took another long pull from the wine bottle.

"I was just trying to find out what she was up to."

"And now you're engaged in a new petty feud, trying to one-up each other," he said. I opened my mouth and immediately closed it. He was right. "It's either that, or you want this goddess gig more than you're letting on."

Maybe he was more right about that than I wanted to admit, too. Honestly, I didn't know which reason compelled me the most, though they felt equally selfish and shameful.

I sighed and dropped my gaze, unable to look him in the eye. "I'm sorry."

Bub's shoulders sagged. "Either way, seems I'll be spending the weekend alone. Cheers." He tilted the wine bottle at me and took another drink before heading inside.

Well, this certainly wasn't how I'd expected the night to end.

Saul licked the back of my hand and whimpered softly. I reached for another cheese cube, then realized he was just letting me know that we had company.

"Is this… a bad time?" Hecate asked, emerging from the shadow of the garden. Her black cloak shimmered under the starlight.

I winced. "How much of that did you hear?"

"Enough to know that you have new shoes and a sexually frustrated demon." She gave me an apologetic smile as she climbed the patio steps.

"That about sums it up," I said, not wanting to re-hash the embarrassing details.

"You're welcome to send him to the grove if his hounding becomes tedious," Hecate offered. "The lampads act as if they're in heat. I recall now a second myth that explained why Gale was transformed into a polecat. She's insatiable. Worse than a succubus, I swear."

I crinkled my nose at the idea. "Thanks, but we'll manage."

"I could also mix a potion that would render him impotent—temporarily, of course," she added at my horror. "It wears off rather quickly. *Too* quickly, in my opinion."

"That's… no thanks." I shook my head, trying to clear it of the subject. Girl talk took a dark turn with chthonic goddesses. "Hey, did you ever walk among the mortals back in your day?" I asked, steering the conversation away from my demon's sex drive.

"Sure, lots of times." Hecate pushed the hood of her cloak back and leaned over the patio table to assess the snacks. "Almost everyone did. I suppose that's why our myths are so scrambled. Many of the gods tried to manipulate the beliefs of mortals to funnel soul matter into their afterlives on this side. They'd change the story according to their audience, tell them whatever they wanted to hear. It was a major cornerstone of the First War of Eternity, and one of the first issues addressed in the treaty."

"Did you try to change your story?" I asked, wondering how much of the goddess was self-made and how much had been left up to mortal dreamers.

Hecate popped a salt-crusted almond into her mouth and cocked her head from side to side. "I was more interested in the witches that already believed in me, the covens that breathed life into my mythos. I enjoyed studying and developing their mysteries."

"That seems like a noble use of your time."

I thought of the nights I'd spent with the Woke Souls. Even if I had the opportunity to manipulate mortals into bolstering my budding deityship, I was pretty sure I'd rather be with the ones who already believed in me, too.

"I visit my mortal followers from time to time," Hecate explained. "Just no longer in the flesh. It's too risky, and there are too many rules. Besides, I brought my talisman back to Eternity before the treaty went into effect."

"Your talisman?" I perked, eager to know more.

"Any god can be inserted into the mortal world through the basic soul insertion process, though they lose their divine memories in those lifetimes, thanks to the treaty. But prior to the war, if you wanted to swap souls with a living mortal—for any length of time outside of a general ritual circle—it involved ceremonies and sacrifices. *Mysteries*. And naturally, blessed tokens that bound you to a mortal vessel for the duration of its life. That's the key—a *real* one, in my case," she said, lifting the key pendant of her necklace that I never saw her without.

"And since you brought it back to Eternity, it no longer works?" I asked, trying to understand how it all worked.

"Not necessarily. It's just a lot harder to return a talisman to the mortal side than it is to retrieve one." She pressed her lips together and tucked the key back under her cloak. "It's much like a soul. Have you ever tried to put one back where you found it?"

"Uh, no." I chuckled at the idea. "Psychopomps only work one way."

Hecate nodded. "And the creation deities are limited by the treaty and soul recycling protocols. I wouldn't be surprised if some have lost their abilities altogether, especially since no new talismans have been issued since the treaty was signed."

"Bummer."

Hecate shrugged. "It's not a wholly terrible thing. Many of the gods had no business playing with the mortals. They launched wars and crusades. Then there were gods like Zeus." She snorted. "He'd hop in *any* living creature, so long as it had a working phallus."

"*Aaand* we're back on this ride."

"Sorry." Hecate grimaced. "I left the grove because I needed a break from all the smut, but I suppose it's going to take more than an hour or two to scrub my mind clean of those visions. I think I need a lengthier vacation."

"You and me both." I sighed and glanced up at the darkened bedroom window behind us. Of course, my vacation would include carnal delights. Just with a single demon instead of a harem of underworld nymphs.

"I better head home." Hecate patted my arm and bent down to scratch Saul under the chin. Coreen had already corralled the helljacks back to the garage. "Seems we both have fires to put out yet tonight."

CHAPTER SEVEN

"Love without sex is still the most
efficient form of hell known to man."
—Peter Porter

I'D EXPECTED TO FIND BUB asleep when I entered our room—or at least *pretending* to sleep. The half-drunk wine bottle sat forgotten on the bedside table, and my demon's face glowed blue in the light of his tablet. He glanced up as I sat on the edge of the bed, but quickly looked back to his screen, jaw setting in a hard line.

"There are several sites in Egypt where archeologists soon hope to discover Cleopatra's tomb," he said stiffly. "I suspect one of them is where Isis's cult stashed her pearly charms. You'll want to pack a hat and good hiking boots—"

"You *could* come with me," I suggested, walking my fingertips up his forearm. "This isn't council business, and I doubt Anubis would take issue. Besides, if this *is* the beginning of my goddess myth, what better way to establish you as my consort?"

"Consort?" Bub pressed a hand to his chest. "Why, Miss Harvey, are you proposing?"

"And if I am?" I asked, brows lifting hopefully. His devilish grin returned, and something fluttered low in my stomach as he leaned forward to kiss me. Maybe the night wouldn't be a total bust.

"Don't the mortals usually do this on their knees?" he whispered against my mouth.

"Is that where you want me?" I slid my tongue over his bottom lip.

"We may need some rope."

A startled laugh caught in my throat, and I blinked at him. "Well, that escalated quickly."

"For Egypt," he clarified, then scrambled out of bed and disappeared inside his closet. "Plus a canteen, compass, flashlight… perhaps a notepad."

"Okay?" I blew into my hand to check my breath, wondering if something in Rupert's charcuterie selection had been laced with garlic.

"Saul would be handy to have along for his nose," Bub's muffled voice called as he ventured deeper. "But we should probably bring Coreen, as well. You know how destructive she gets when she's left behind."

"Sure." I rolled over and unfastened the scarab belt before shimmying out of my dress. Lacy panties would get things back on track.

"Rupert can tend to Ursula and your apprentice's beasts while we're away," Bub went on. "The garden should keep if we're only a day or two."

"I know a garden that could use some tending right now," I said, striking a pose across the bedspread as my demon finally exited the closet.

"Hmmm?" He spared me an appreciative ogle and then vanished again, this time into my closet. "Watering *your* rose bush will have to wait too, love. We should get a good night's sleep. The desert is no place to arrive unawares."

I groaned and buried my face in the pillows. "We'll have coin to get around. We're not exploring the Sahara on camels."

"Speaking of coin," Bub said, ignoring my whining. "Don't forget the extra special one you've been saving for emergencies. You know the one I mean?"

"Of course," I snapped. "I never leave home without it. What sort of idiot do you take me for?"

Bub poked his head out of the closet and frowned at my crumpled bottom lip. "I'm sorry, pet. The last-second planning has me in a tizzy. I meant no offense." He hung my overnight bag on the door hook and sat on the edge of the bed. "We'll celebrate properly on our return. Perhaps you can take off an extra day or two. The death rate on the mortal side is in a lull, and your apprentices are competent enough to manage things on their own for a bit."

"Fine." I dragged myself off the bed and fished a pair of yoga pants and a tank top out of my dresser. "You really think this could take all weekend?" I asked. I hadn't considered the possibility when I was determined to turn Isis down.

"There are a lot of historic sites in Egypt," Bub said, nudging me aside to dig a pair of socks and underwear out of the drawer above my pajamas. "And graverobbing has been a problem for ages, so they went to some extreme measures to conceal the tombs of their most revered pharaohs and their treasures."

"Do *you* have any treasure hidden on the mortal side? Any fancy talisman crafted by Satanic cults so you could go skin-walking among them?" I cocked my head, marveling at how little I knew about his past.

"There are a few trinkets scattered about, though nothing quite on par with Isis's pearls." Bub finished packing my bag as I dressed for bed, and then he turned to face me, brow furrowed in thought. "I've been summoned to my fair share of ritual circles, and I punched the possession time clock for a good while, but few demons live out lengthy lifetimes in mortal flesh. The fiery nature of our soul matter complicates matters. A bit too caustic for feeble human bodies, I'm afraid."

"Do you think Grim ever lived among the mortals?" I asked.

"Why?" Bub crossed the room and took my hands in his. "Please don't tell me you're considering leaving Eternity to live out a mortal life for the sake of crafting your myth. I don't fancy being a long-distance consort. If this was meant to be a consolation prize—"

"No, no." I shook my head. "I was just curious. You know, made in Grim's image and all."

Bub tucked a curl behind my ear and cupped my face. "Perhaps you were made in his image, but your myth is your own. And it's unique. The first and only of its kind, born of believers on this side of the grave. Don't let anyone convince you that you're anything less than phenomenal."

I pressed my cheek into his hand and sighed. "I hope you're wrong about it taking all weekend. I was really looking forward to the quality time with you."

"As was I with you." Bub clicked his tongue. "But we'll still be together in Egypt."

"True. And I'm sure your demonic talents will speed things along."

"Well…" He winced at the praise. "Sadly, my skills are limited outside of Eternity. Here the soul matter may be stabilized, but on the mortal side, we demons only have as much power as belief allows."

"What?" I gaped at him, wondering how in the world I had missed such a seemingly vital detail. To be fair, my training at the Reaper Academy had focused on honing my own abilities, and reapers very rarely worked with other beings.

"It's all right, love." Bub stroked my arm. "We've never spent enough time together on the mortal side for it to matter."

"But reapers don't have a religion," I said, not sure what to make of the new information. "I mean, we don't have the ability to burst into a swarm of flies or anything, but I've never had to worry about losing my skill set."

"Your ability to harvest souls is quite impressive," Bub countered. "I can only retrieve one that's been bartered away and marked for Hell. It's not the same at all."

"I don't understand."

"Well… How to explain…" He licked the corner of his mouth. "Reapers, like Grim, descend from a universal, primordial entity. *Death*. One of the two most powerful forces in the universe—the other being life or creation. Together, they serve as the veil between worlds. Your abilities reflect that, and no matter a mortal's religious affiliation, they all believe in life and death. And so, they believe in you."

"But people believe in demons, too," I said.

"Yes, some people do still believe in demons," Bub agreed. "Just not like they used to back in the Middle

Ages or even during the Satanic Panic of the eighties. And the demon you see before you is not the variety many mortals will recognize in Egypt. Unless I'm interacting with a mortal who's summoned me or I have a permit to possess, my talents are stunted."

"Oh." My nose crinkled in frustration. No wonder he was going overboard with the supplies. We might actually need them.

"Don't fret," Bub said, patting the top of my hand. "I'll be plenty useful in other ways. And I'm sure Anubis will have packed any necessities we've forgotten—oh! Your axe! I didn't see it in the closet."

"I left it on the ship. I was anticipating a relaxing weekend," I explained at his confused scowl.

"Well, I guess we can drop by the harbor in the morning before meeting with Anubis."

"What? No. I am not dragging that thing through cramped temple corridors all weekend." I huffed and flopped back onto the bed.

Bub threw his arms up in disbelief. "The culprit who was rallying hellcats to the mortal side is still out there, with a rather large grudge, I'm sure. You slew the scoundrel's steed and cut off their favorite recruiting passages."

"Yeah, but isn't that lot over in Iraq, between the Tigris and Euphrates, or wherever Sumer used to be?"

"Not necessarily," Bub said. "The Egyptian gods didn't just mingle with the Greeks and Romans, and Isis wasn't the only deity with a foreign consort."

I blew a raspberry at him and burrowed under the covers. "We're going to a crusty old temple. No one even knows we'll be there."

"I'm at least packing your throwing stars." He lifted his chin, daring me to challenge him again as he stalked off to my closet once more.

"Can I have the boot daggers instead?" I shouted.

Bub made a dejected noise, and then something fell off a shelf and he swore. "The stars were a gift—from me. I can't believe you don't like them."

"I do! It's just…" I groaned. "They're hell on my legs, especially if there's any climbing involved."

"Fine." He stepped out of the closet and tucked my pair of daggers down in the front pocket of my bag so I wouldn't forget them in the morning. His other hand rubbed the top of his head gingerly. "That's an accepta-ble compromise, seeing as how I intend to be all the hell your legs can handle."

"Just not tonight?" I pouted, though my begging was interrupted by a long yawn.

Bub peeled back the covers and settled in next to me. He laid his head on the pillow beside mine, his grin sof-tening as my eyes grew heavy and closed. I felt his hand brush a curl away from my face.

"We'll have more nights," he whispered.

"I want them all."

"They're yours."

"Because you're my consort?" I asked. "You never answered earlier."

"I've been yours from the very beginning. If you need to make it official, show me where to sign. I'll use my own blood and every name that's ever been uttered to summon me."

"We don't need bloody contracts. But maybe one of those cakes with the little people on top?"

"Whatever my lover goddess desires."

"Nothing too fancy. Rupert can make it," I added, my voice trailing off along with my consciousness.

"Do you want me to stuff it in your face like the humans do?" Bub asked, his words gently fading.

I giggled at the question, my tired brain unable to muster a response. And then sleep and dreams took over.

CHAPTER EIGHT

"I wonder if other dogs think poodles
are members of a weird religious cult."
—Rita Rudner

THE STYX STOP NEAR THE GATES OF HELL was quiet this early in the day. It would be busier come lunchtime, when the more ambitious reapers ventured through to unload their morning harvests. For the breakfast crowd, a single spade-tailed waitress was enough for the half dozen demons scattered throughout the diner. And the one Egyptian god lounging in the booth nearest the door.

"Manto," I said to Saul and Coreen, pointing them toward a shady spot along the side of the building before Bub and I headed inside. A bell above the door announced our arrival, and the smell of greasy eggs and strong coffee greeted us.

Anubis glanced up and back down at his newspaper. Then he did a double take. "Lana! You came."

I hitched a brow at him. "You seem surprised."

"I am," he admitted. Then his gaze snagged on Bub, standing a step behind me. "And you brought your… lover."

"Soon-to-be-consort," Bub countered.

"Is that a problem?" I dropped my travel bag in the booth and rested a hand on my hip. It was a little soon in the adventure for trouble, but I was irritated enough about having my weekend ruined that I was ready to spit nails if he gave me any grief.

"Not at all. The more the merrier, right?" Anubis offered up a tight smile and shook his paper at the table. "Come. Sit. Let's get some coffee in you and go over the agenda."

Agenda. That sounded nice and time-consuming. I began to wonder if it was too late to back out. Of course, this early in the morning, I questioned the logic of doing *anything* that wasn't absolutely necessary. We were definitely going to need coffee.

Bub looped the straps of his backpack over the corner of the bench seat and waited for me to scooch in against the window. Outside, morning light filtered through the brimstone smog rising from the Styx. I hoped the wind would cooperate and blow it the opposite direction, far away from my hounds whose thick coats absorbed stink like nobody's business.

A staticky radio crooned through the kitchen service window, blaring the latest and greatest hits of the underworld according to the Fallen Frequency Radio Station. Between songs, the show host detailed the sinfully mild weather we'd be missing out on this weekend. Perfect conditions for lust, sloth, and gluttony. I'd been looking forward to all three.

"What'll ya have?" the waitress asked, finally making her way over to our table. She repeated Anubis's double take, but at Bub this time instead of me. "I'm so sorry for the wait," she stammered, spiky tail curling between her legs. "Whatever you'd like, it's on the house, Your Profane Darkness."

"That's quite all right," Bub assured her, doffing his straw fedora. I left mine on to fend off the sunlight spilling through the window. "Two coffees please, dressed up with all the sweets," Bub requested.

"Right away." The waitress bowed and scampered off, echoing more apologies as she went.

"Such service," Anubis noted dryly, frowning down at his empty mug.

Without his jackal headdress and gilded ceremony attire, it was hard to place him as a god. The casual, white tunic shirt and sandals made him look more like a local tour guide about to take us sightseeing.

"Anyway," he said, huffing a dejected sigh. "We'll be coming in at Dendera. Sekhmet is waiting there to lead us through the Temple of Hathor in search of a scroll that belonged to Isis's kin cult before they dispersed."

"Kin cult?" Bub inquired, saving me the trouble.

"Descendants of Cleopatra, Isis's last mortal vessel," Anubis explained. "Her many-times-great-granddaughter, Drusilla Selene, returned the pearl halves to Egypt in the fourth century and gathered the cult one last time to move Cleopatra's tomb from the island of Antirhodos before it sank into the Mediterranean. The location of her final resting place, along with her talisman, is thought to be documented in the scroll hidden within the Temple of Hathor."

"Excuse me?" I snapped. "Isis said she already knew where the pearl halves were."

"She does—sort of." Anubis hesitated as the waitress reappeared with two enormous mugs topped with whipped cream and caramel syrup. She set them on the table along with a plate of donut holes. My stomach leapt at the promise of so much sugar. "Uh, could I get another?" Anubis asked as the waitress turned to leave.

"Sure." She fetched a pot from behind the counter and refilled his mug. I waited for him to take a drink before resuming the grilling.

"Do you know where the talisman is or not?" I demanded. "I am not about to run all over Egypt if you only *sort of* know where we're going."

"Cleopatra's tomb is at Taposiris Magna, west of Alexandria." Anubis lowered his voice and shot a nervous glance around the café. "But there are many tunnels and dead ends beneath the temple ruins. It floods regularly, and the structure is unstable. It's a dangerous place to be if you don't know precisely where you're going. The scroll is said to mark the exact location of the tomb."

I squinted at him. "And Sekhmet knows where this scroll is?"

"Eh." He shrugged. "More or less."

"Then why is it not already in her possession?" Bub asked, folding his arms. Though the whipped cream on the end of his nose took something away from his scolding demeanor.

"It contains a mystery of Isis." Anubis rolled his eyes as if everyone knew what that meant. "The seal cannot be broken by any other deity of our pantheon without grave consequence. And since you'll be on hand anyway, I didn't see any reason to include another member in this party." He shot Bub a sideways glance. "No offense. It's just a very delicate situation."

"Fair enough." I paused to slurp at my coffee sundae and stuffed a donut hole in my mouth. "I'm still confused why you can't harvest the talisman yourself. Aren't you a psychopomp?"

Anubis's face flushed, but I couldn't tell if he was embarrassed or angered by the question. "I'd love to, honestly. But my faith is too diminished on the mortal side. I lost the ability to guide souls to Duat a long time ago. We rely solely on the reapers now. Many of the older faiths do."

"Sore subject, I take it." Bub finished his coffee and slid his empty mug aside before turning to me. "Well, love? Are you intent on seeing this through?"

I glanced between him and Anubis, feeling the weight of the question. This little quest was more involved than I'd realized. Despite my pride and reluctance to jump on the goddess bandwagon, I wanted Isis's blessing. I wanted to please Cordelia and the Woke Souls. I wanted Bub as my official consort. And I definitely wanted to rub the lost opportunity in Tasha's face.

"Let's hit the dusty trail," I said, committing to the half-baked plan.

"That's the spirit!" Anubis lifted his mug in a silent toast before polishing it off in two swallows. Then he dropped a coin on the table and stood. Bub placed a coin on the table too, even though the waitress had insisted our drinks were on the house. He palmed a second coin in preparation of our departure. Then he gathered up his hat and our bags, and we followed Anubis outside.

It was always hot along the banks of the Styx, but in the early hours of the morning, it was almost bearable. It was a shame we had to leave. I dug a coin out of my pocket and clicked my tongue at the hounds, signaling them to gather in close enough for our auras to touch so they wouldn't be left behind. Meanwhile, Anubis put his hands on his waist and twisted from side to side, stretching his back. I wondered what the holdup was, until a pair of jackals materialized.

Coreen let out an excited yip and immediately stuck her nose under the nearest dog's tail. He reciprocated as the other jackal waited for his turn.

"Whoa, whoa, whoa." I shooed them away. "Break it up."

"They're just saying hello." Anubis chuckled at my prudish protests.

"Yeah, and we all know where that leads." I shot Coreen a dirty look. "If you start popping out puppies again, I'm sending you to live with Hades and Persephone."

"My antique furniture will not tolerate the abuse of your adorable abominations," Bub added sternly.

Anubis pressed his lips together, suppressing his amusement when our ire turned on him. "Come along, boys," he called the jackals, patting his leg. With his other hand, he held up a coin. "Onward, to the land of the living."

CHAPTER NINE

"In ancient times cats were worshipped as gods;
they have not forgotten this."
—*Terry Pratchett*

THOUGH EGYPTIAN ARABIC was the dominant language in Egypt, a sizable chunk of the population spoke English. Which meant I'd been approved for a harvest here and there in recent years.

The classes I'd taken to prepare for the Posy Unit had added a few new territories to my resume and leveled me up to medium-risk souls. If the Fates needed an extra reaper in Egypt, I usually found myself in one of the bigger cities, Cairo or Luxor, and I rarely ventured beyond the hospitals, wash rooms, and cemeteries where my harvests took place. I'd never had the time to stop and smell the monuments.

Spring in southern Egypt was only slightly cooler than hell. By summer, it would be hard to tell them apart. I was hopeful we'd have Isis's cult scroll in hand and be off to Alexandria before the sun baked us to a crisp—or melted the snacks Rupert had tucked inside our bags.

The temperature didn't seem to bother our canine companions, even with their dark, heat-absorbing fur. Tartarus and Duat had similar climates, lush oases scattered across arid stretches of desert. Of course, our plot of land on the banks of the Styx in Tartarus had a more diabolic odor to it. At least if Saul decided to roll around in this sand, he wouldn't come away smelling like rotten eggs.

A headless sphinx lounged outside the crumbling entrance of the Dendera temple complex. The towering pylon featured engraved images of ancient pharaohs, but the gate built across its threshold was modern, designed to keep tourists away in the off-hours. It had already been opened for the day, and a handful of people waited in line to gain entry. We slipped by them unnoticed and continued past the rows of broken statues and engraved blocks on display.

The mudbrick wall around the complex enclosed several buildings, but it was the largest of these that Anubis led us toward. It was an intimidating structure. Not as recognizable as the pyramids of Giza or the Great Sphinx, but the classic Egyptian architecture was impressive.

Six enormous columns spanned the facade of the temple. They were squared off at the top with faces carved on all four sides, the features of each one mutilated. The figures' hair and little fluted cow ears had mostly survived the defacing, enough so that it was clearly the same goddess on each column.

"The Temple of Hathor," Anubis announced with a wave of his hand. I'd never met Hathor, so I supposed I wouldn't have recognized her even if her many faces hadn't been disfigured.

There were plenty of ancient deities I had not met, and for a variety of reasons. Some were content with retirement and enjoyed quieter lives since fading into obscurity. Those who bored of that opted for reinsertion on the mortal side to live out human lives, their soul matter completing the circle of faith. And then there were the ones who had perished in the First War of Eternity. I wasn't entirely sure where Hathor had fallen through the cracks, and I was never one to leave well enough alone.

"If it's Hathor's temple, why are we meeting Sekhmet?" I asked, scrutinizing the people scattered throughout the courtyard. The goddess of bloodlust and intoxication didn't seem like the type one should risk offending.

Anubis chuckled. "I forget how young you reapers are sometimes."

"Yeah, yeah." I rolled my eyes. "We're the new kids on the immortal block."

He diverted his patronizing grin away from me before answering my question. "Ra turned Hathor into Sekhmet during the First War of Eternity. Not for the first time, but certainly the last."

"Like how Parvati can transform into Kali?" I said, earning a surprised look from Bub.

The highlights of the war had been covered in the history class I'd taken as part of my initial training at the Reaper Academy over three hundred years ago. Kali had been a major fixture on the battlefields, but there had been mention of a few Egyptian deities too, like Horus and Ammit. A warrior goddess like Sekhmet had surely been among them.

"Right." Anubis nodded. "Except Parvati still has many believers who enable her to smoothly transition between forms. Hathor… was not so lucky. She has remained Sekhmet ever since. Ra was unable to change her back."

"Did he run out of beer?" I asked, recalling Jack's note about the goddess when she'd briefly been a suspect during the hellcat exodus. Ra had once fed her red-dyed booze to sate her bloodlust after she'd gotten carried away on a revenge mission.

"I imagine." Anubis snorted. "But alas, the lioness remains. They say it was this failure of Ra's that led him to abandon Duat and join the mortal coil."

Well, that explained why I'd never met Hathor, but it presented another more important question. Bub beat me to it.

"Sekhmet's familiar with this temple though, yes?" He frowned at Anubis and readjusted the bag hanging from his shoulder. "We're not just crossing our fingers and hoping this trip down memory lane jogs loose something useful, are we?"

"Such little faith." Anubis shook his head and marched on toward another modern gate that marked the entrance to the temple. His jackals kept pace, though one glanced back at Coreen.

"*Such little faith*," Bub echoed in a dopey voice. Then he leaned in and whispered over my shoulder. "Give me a wink, love, and I'll fake a sprained ankle or migraine so we can bow out of this nonsense."

"Shhh," I hissed at his teasing and nudged him away before relieving him of my bag. The gentleman act was endearing, but I was no prima donna. I ignored Bub's grumbling and hurried to catch up with Anubis. The hounds trotted alongside me, tongues lolling and tails wagging.

A low wall stretched between the temple columns. Above, the Hathor heads were connected by screens that gave a view of the vestibule beyond and more defaced pillars. The happy chirps of birds echoed within, despite the barrier. They'd found their own secret entrance to access the shade and nesting nooks the temple offered.

Several tourists lingered outside, waiting in line at the gate. But only one noticed us.

I couldn't decide if she was over or underdressed, with her fringe-lined halter top and matching red skirt. Golden cobra cuffs hugged her biceps, and rings lined nearly every finger and toe. Two dark braids laid over her shoulders, dotted with more gold and tiny gemstones, and a large pendant hung from a chain around her neck. All the finery drew my attention to her shoeless feet crusted with sand.

I had a moment of hesitation wherein I considered the possibility that she was an eccentric original believer, but then the sun caught her eyes. Narrow slits dilated in the crimson pools of her irises, like black roses blooming inside a furnace.

"The Master of Secrets himself." Sekhmet curtseyed at Anubis. It was a playful, mocking gesture rather than one of respect.

"Mistress of Dread," Anubis replied, bowing in similar fashion. Their banter was strained, like cousins at a family reunion, timidly trying on old nicknames that no longer fit. I'd collected a soul or two from such events—and over sillier discrepancies.

Sekhmet looked me up and down. "This is the reaper banished to Hell?" she said with a hint of awe. *Joy*, a rebel fetish.

"Eh, no—" Anubis gave me an apologetic smile. "This is Lana Harvey, the reaper recommended by Horus."

Sekhmet's fiery stare shifted to Bub and then back to me. "The would-be goddess with the demonic lover?"

"I see my reputation precedes me," I said dryly.

Sekhmet made a strange sound that crossed between a purr and a growl, and I realized that was her idea of a snicker. "I was told you had refused to do the *Queen of the Throne's* bidding," she said, voice dripping with more disdain. Her gaze dropped to the hounds. "A dog person. That explains it."

"Explains what?" I scoffed, daring her to launch an insult at dogs while Anubis and his jackals stood among us.

"Why you're so eager to please," Sekhmet cooed. "We cat people are our own masters."

"Is that so?" I folded my arms. "If you're not interested in pleasing Isis or doing her bidding, why are you helping us?"

Sekhmet's red eyes narrowed, but then she grinned. "Touché, reaper." She waved her arm good-naturedly toward the temple gate, now empty of patrons. "Come along. I'll show you where I think the scroll may be hiding."

As she turned away, Anubis patted my shoulder. "Forgive the ribbing. Sek's combative nature is confined to words these days. Don't let her get under your skin just because she's stuck in hers."

Egyptian deities seemed to be good at that, and it never ended well—for either party. I'd have to work harder to keep my cool today, in spite of the desert heat *and* the cheeky goddess.

"I've tolerated worse." I shrugged and headed inside. Bub and the hounds followed close behind, leaving Anubis and his jackals to bring up the rear of our search party.

It was cooler in the shade of the temple, though the air felt solemn, as if it remembered every prayer uttered within these sacred walls. The enormous pillars and high ceilings were covered in hieroglyphs and bas-reliefs, some painted with vibrant colors that had remarkably endured the millennia.

More ancient designs were scrawled across the walls, images of gods and pharaohs carved in between rows of strange symbols, with an occasional animal, eyeball, or lotus flower. I twisted a slow circle, overwhelmed by the beauty and mystery of it all.

Anubis craned his neck and pointed out a narrow swath of ceiling that was stained black. "It's been some years, but it all looked like that when I last visited. Desert squatters and early Christians fleeing persecution took shelter here, after the temple had been abandoned. Their fires covered the sandstone with soot. They're to blame for the vandalism, as well."

"Insolent, filthy mortals. Imagine that." Sekhmet snorted. "Then Napoleon's scavengers stole the sky disk from Osiris's chapel on the roof and replaced it with a fake."

"Ah, yes," Bub said. "The original is in the Louvre. That's where I've heard of this temple."

Anubis sighed. "Museum fodder. I suppose that's all our temples and treasures are good for now."

Sadly, he was right. Not many ancient holy places had stood the test of time. Those that had survived were little more than ruins maintained to draw in tourist revenue. Though few could boast the splendor of Hathor's temple, where every inch was a divine masterpiece—perfect for photo ops.

"This way," Sekhmet instructed, leading us past a herd of girls taking selfies. "They've opened another crypt beneath the temple, but there's a hidden chamber they've yet to discover."

The hall beyond featured more pillars, though it was smaller and lined with numerous rooms. From what I could see as we hurried past, each one was just as decorated as the vestibule, with floor-to-ceiling hieroglyphs and illustrations. Some were dark, lit only by thin daylight spilling through high, tiny windows. Others were illuminated by bright floor lights pressed up against the walls.

The next room we entered was even smaller and lacked the elaborate pillars. I spotted a stairway and more empty rooms before we carried on to the next antechamber. Here we finally paused, the path Sekhmet had been blazing blocked by a larger, central shrine. A narrow hallway curled around it, but the goddess cut right, heading for an adjacent room. As we passed, she shot a dirty look down the corridor running along the right side of the shrine. An arched doorway to a room at the back of the temple lent a view of a wooden railing around an opening in the floor.

Sekhmet's nose crinkled with distaste. "Sacred spaces once known only to the holiest of attendants, now open to the entire world like roadside attractions."

I supposed that was why Isis was so eager to reclaim her talisman. Modern technology was more advanced than any of us had anticipated—despite mortal fairytales of flying cars and robot servants. The humans were uncovering more hidden places and ancient secrets every day.

The new room we entered revealed a passage back to the stairs I'd noticed in the previous antechamber. It also held a doorway to a surprisingly sunny chapel. The once open ceiling was covered in glass windows. More reliefs and hieroglyphs decorated the walls, though most of the finer details had been chiseled away like elsewhere in the temple.

A short stairway led up to an area flanked by a pair of smaller Hathor pillars, but we didn't make it that far. Sekhmet stopped at a wooden railing wrapped around another opening in the floor. A locked gate kept obedient guests from accessing this crypt entrance. I assumed a qualified guide was required.

"Ladies first," Anubis said, waving a hand at Sekhmet. She gathered up her skirt and climbed over the railing, balancing on the ladder below. Anubis turned to me next.

"I don't see a light down there." I frowned at the shadows puddling beneath Sekhmet as she descended. The goddess's face tilted up, and her gaze met mine, eyes glowing like embers.

"I can see in the dark," she said with a sharp smile.

Bub cleared his throat and tugged me back a step by the strap of my bag before unzipping one of the pockets and producing a flashlight. He tutted at my obvious relief.

"You didn't think I made such a fuss over preparations last night for nothing, did you?"

"Thank you," I replied in lieu of the truth. Then I tucked the flashlight under one arm and climbed over the railing as Sekhmet had. Once clear of the ladder, Bub and Anubis made a show of leaping over the railing and stirred up a cloud of dust with their landings. The hounds and jackals were next, thickening the sallow hue of the air.

I coughed and edged away, following Sekhmet deeper into the crypt.

A narrow tunnel split off to the left, no wider than the thickness of the temple walls. If I'd been claustrophobic, this would have been a deal-breaker. Saul nudged the back of my leg, and I swore as my elbow grazed a rough patch in the stone wall.

"Careful, reaper," Sekhmet purred, her fiery eyes zeroing in on me. "Blood is a popular catalyst for ancient spells, and there are many on these walls."

Bub, true to form, dug a bandage out of his pack and doctored the abrasion. He snuck a kiss while our divine companions assessed a gap in the stones opposite the passage I assumed we'd be taking.

I shined my flashlight between them, into a chamber below. The space wasn't much longer than a coffin. It was also a dead-end, unless you counted the hole along the base of the left side wall. It looked just big enough to squeeze a body through if one were trying to cover up a murder, and I would know. I'd harvested my fair share of homicide victims from similar dumping sites.

The glow of my flashlight shifted to Anubis and Sekhmet, and I glared at them. "You *must* be joking."

"What's the problem now, reaper?" Sekhmet asked, aiming her feline eyes at me.

"*That* is the problem," I said, circling the beam of the flashlight around the hole. "Spelunking is Recovery Unit territory. I'm not qualified for this bullshit."

"Good to know." Sekhmet snorted. "However, we'll be going the other way—" I managed half a sigh of relief before she added, "—through the opposite wall."

"Come again?" I angled the flashlight into the room once more, wondering what I'd missed.

"It rotates." Sekhmet made a V with her hands in an attempt to show how it worked and earned a blank stare for the effort. "You'll see. Though it is a tight fit, so you'll want to leave your *luggage* out here."

"What about the hounds?" I asked, eying Coreen and her proximity to Anubis's jackals.

"They'll have to stay behind, too," Sekhmet said. "Perhaps your demon can watch over them?"

"I think not." Bub dropped his bag near the ladder up to the chapel and lifted his chin. "I go where she goes."

I made another face at Coreen but resisted asking Bub to reconsider. Our adventures were too few these days to expect him to sit on the sidelines. How could I offer him the title of consort and then refuse to include him in my so-called myth?

I dropped my bag beside Bub's and pointed a finger at the hounds. "*Manto.*"

Coreen sat and licked her nose, but I didn't miss the sideways glance she gave the jackals. She would have to be taken back to the manor at lunchtime. There was just no way around it. The mangled couch cushions and shoes from one of her tantrums was nothing compared to what a litter of helljacks would do to our home.

Sekhmet took the lead again, climbing over the stone ledge and into the tiny chamber. She pressed herself against the far end, making way for Anubis next. On my first attempt to join them, I mangled my hat on the narrow opening and nearly fell in.

Bub took the straw fedora from me and discarded it along with his own on top of our bags. Then he held the flashlight as I lowered myself into the room with more care, passing it back as soon as I'd found my footing.

The creepy hole was too close for comfort. I shined the light at it, but there was nothing to see at such an awkward angle. Still, visions of snakes and spiders filled my head. I squished in tighter beside Anubis, ignoring Sekhmet's grunt of displeasure as I pushed him into her to make enough space for Bub. I somehow doubted this many bodies were meant to be in here at once.

Hot breath filled the air between us, and what had begun as a cool underground crypt was quickly becoming a sauna. My pulse kicked in my throat while Sekhmet patted down the stone wall, searching for whatever secret lever or button would get things moving.

"Here we are," she finally announced. A moment passed in which nothing happened. "Maybe this is it," she said, touching a different spot. "Or perhaps the four of us weigh too much for the contraption to work."

"Nonsense." Bub huffed and shoved a shoulder into the wall. "I'm sure it's just old and needs a little elbow grease."

"Yeah," I agreed, leaning my back against the small space I occupied. I propped a foot against the opposite wall, using it as leverage.

"I felt something!" Anubis braced both feet above the hole and grunted. Then the room trembled, and everything went sideways.

CHAPTER TEN

"Life lasts but a few scratches of the claw in the sand."
—Wislawa Szymborska

I HAD ENVISIONED THE WALL rotating from side to side, like a revolving door at a hotel. Instead, it folded inward, flipping us ass over elbows into a secret room on the other side.

The stone slab we'd pushed in had become part of the floor. And the floor we'd been standing on rose up at our backs. Dust and debris spilled in after us, billowing into a choking cloud. I tucked my face in the bend of my elbow and coughed as I blinked the grit from my eyes.

"All right, love?" Bub asked, touching my arm. I wrapped a hand around his elbow and let him pull me to my feet.

"I dropped the flashlight," I confessed. Thankfully, we didn't need it.

Red orbs fixed to the opposite wall illuminated the room in hellish hues. It was twice the width of the last, and twice as long. Which still didn't make for a very large space. Though the reliefs were in better shape here, untouched by the hands of ancient zealots.

"There are seven sun disks," Sekhmet said, her attention already returned to the task at hand.

Anubis pushed past her to begin at the far side of the room. He squinted at the hieroglyphs, mumbling to himself as he read. The glowing orbs—sun disks, as Sekhmet had called them—were high up on the wall. They all rested within the horned headdresses of seven life-sized reliefs spaced between the columns and rows of symbols.

"Is that… Isis?" I asked, noting the throne each figure sat upon and the wings extending from their arms.

"Yes," Sekhmet answered. Her voice was soft and laced with a growl. "An untrained eye might mistake them for the Seven Hathors, but you see the scorpions in her laps? They are the seven who protected Isis as she reared Horus in the marshes, hidden away from Seth."

My eyes scanned the wall again, this time taking in the scorpion perched in the lap of each Isis relief. There were so many tiny details. It was hard to appreciate them all in a single glance.

"They all look the same to me," Bub said.

"Yes, the images are identical," Anubis agreed. "The clue to which one possesses the scroll must be hidden within the text, among the many names of the goddess."

"What do you mean *possesses*?" I hitched a brow at him. "Where could they possibly be hiding anything? Up a sleeve?"

"Another secret chamber, perhaps?" Bub offered, inspecting his corner of the room.

"The sun disks." Sekhmet held her hand close to one of the glowing orbs, letting its light reflect over her skin. It was slightly larger than a grapefruit. "The Eye of Ra," she said. "Isis tricked my father out of his true name, and now her daughters have hidden her mortal legacy behind a riddle of names we must unravel."

"How does it work then?" I asked, timidly touching the nearest orb. It was warm. Too warm. The room was heating up quickly, and I suddenly realized that my hair was damp with sweat. If we didn't figure this out soon, we were going to suffocate in here.

Anubis licked his lips and traced a finger over a symbol above the first sun disk. "This here mentions *Matet*, one of the seven scorpions. Perhaps the answer lies with them."

"No." I shook my head and sucked in an unbearable breath of hot air. "I mean, how do we get the scroll out? Do these things twist, or just—" I pressed in on the one under my hand, and it made a sharp clicking noise.

"Wait!" Sekhmet shouted. But it was too late.

The orb shot out as if spring-loaded, revealing itself to be the end of a heavy, leather scroll case. It dropped into my open hands.

"That wasn't so hard." I wheezed out a clipped laugh, amazed at my luck. It didn't last long.

"Do you hear that?" Anubis asked, squinting up at the ceiling as a hissing sound echoed through the room. Then sand began to pour from the new hole in the wall.

"Put it back!" Bub shouted.

I fumbled with the scroll case, struggling to hold it despite the onslaught of sand pelting my arms and face. "I'm trying!"

"It won't work," Sekhmet snapped. "Just open it. Maybe there's something inside we can use."

I stepped away from the wall and flipped the case over in my hands. A red wax seal held the leather cover in place. I dug my fingernails under it and tore the flap open.

"Nothing?" I gaped in disbelief at the empty cavity. How perfectly useless.

"Let me see that." Anubis snatched the case from me, but I didn't care. I was already turning back to the wall.

"It's got to be in one of them, right?" I said, pressing another sun disk to release the case it held. Sekhmet grabbed my shoulder and yanked me away from the wall.

My back slammed into the one we'd fallen through, and I grunted as the air left my lungs.

"What the hell do you think you're doing?" the goddess snarled. "You're going to kill us all."

"Get a grip." I shrugged her off and opened the new case to discover it was empty as well. "If we find the scroll, we can just coin out of here."

"No, we can't." She grabbed my arm again, stopping me from reaching a third orb. "These walls are covered in spells, you idiot. Coin travel doesn't work down here."

My stomach flopped as the second hole began to spill sand. The floor was already covered with it.

"Then we'll go back the way we came," Bub said, slamming his shoulder into the trick wall.

"That won't work either," Anubis shouted, eyes still glued to the hieroglyphs. His fingers danced over the text, aiding his search. "The trap has been triggered. There is only one way out now."

"You mean—" My mouth fell open, unable to finish the sentence.

"Yes," Sekhmet said. "We either solve the riddle or die trying."

Sand tickled my calves as it spilled over the tops of my boots. With two spouts, it was filling the room even faster. At this rate, we'd be up to our necks in no time. I yanked one foot up and tried to step on top of the sand, immediately sinking again when I lifted my other boot.

"Bloody hell," Bub swore as he attempted the same and cracked his head on the low ceiling.

"Yes," Anubis rasped, tapping his finger above the second glowing orb. "*Tefen.* The scorpions are each mentioned by name."

"What does that mean?" I demanded.

"I don't know, but it must be significant. The names of the goddess are unchanged and in the same order."

I gritted my teeth and squeezed the scroll case in my hand. With nothing more useful to do, I gave it another onceover. The stone cap that had posed as Isis's sun disk no longer glowed with supernatural light. Another smooth stone served as a cap at the opposite end, only this one was dark blue.

"What about this?" I asked, shoving it in Anubis's face. "This is different, right?"

The god's eyes widened hopefully. The first case was clutched in his hand. He held it up for comparison, revealing a matching dark blue stone.

"Lapis lazuli," Sekhmet said, her brow pinching as she looked back to the wall. "The sun disks are carnelian—blood of Isis."

Anubis nodded. "And lapis lazuli was said to hold a spark of her soul, like the talisman."

"Super," I snapped. "How does that help us?" I opened the scroll case again, shaking it upside down as if it would somehow produce an answer like a Magic 8 Ball.

"Wait!" Bub caught my wrist and lifted the broken wax seal, holding the flap up to one of the glowing orbs so the inside of the case was lit. Straight on, I'd miss it. But at the right angle, a series of tiny symbols could be seen, carved into the leather of the inner wall.

Sekhmet pressed in beside me to have a closer look. Her pupils had dilated, the black eating away at her irises until only a ring of fire remained around each.

"What does that say?" I shouted over the hissing rush of sand. It was already past my knees, sucking at my boots each time I tried to move.

"*Petet*," Sekhmet answered in between panting breaths. "Another of the scorpions. Though *Tetet* is the one mentioned above the Isis from which you pulled that case."

"Where does it say *Petet*?" I asked, scanning the hieroglyphs in search of matching symbols.

Sekhmet braced herself against the wall with one hand and dragged herself past me to the Isis relief in front of Bub. "Here," she said, tapping above the glowing sun disk.

"I have *Befen*," Anubis announced, reading the inscription inside his scroll case. "That must be it. We have to match them to the corresponding scorpions."

"Easier said than done when the holes start spitting sand," I said.

"Yes, but it did not begin flowing right away," Bub noted. "Perhaps we should attempt a swifter exchange this time?"

"Seriously?" Sekhmet sneered at him as if he'd suggested we tunnel our way out with spoons. "You think we're in any position to be playing guessing games?"

"Do you have a better idea?" Bub said.

I didn't wait for a reply. I shot my hand out and pressed the orb beneath the name Sekhmet had identified. She spun around and hissed in furious surprise as the scroll case zipped past her face. I ignored her and shoved the matching case into the hole—only for it to instantly spring back out and drop between us. I snatched it up before the falling sand could bury it.

"Perfect!" Sekhmet shrieked. "I'm going to die surrounded by idiots."

CHAPTER ELEVEN

"Three things cannot be long hidden:
the sun, the moon, and the truth."
—*Buddha*

I WAS TOO ANXIOUS TO BE OFFENDED. My heart hammered in my ears, and the cases quivered in my shaking hands.

"Turn it around," Anubis said, swirling his finger in the air. "Lapis lazuli facing out. Quickly!"

I swallowed my panic and did as he instructed. This time, something clicked inside the wall, and the case stayed put. The blue stone flickered to life, its pale light bleeding into our shrinking inferno. I laughed, though my nerves made it sound more like a whimper.

Anubis matched his scroll case to the third relief and swapped it with the one hidden behind Isis's sun disk. More blue light cut into the red, though sand continued to fill the chamber. It slithered between the buttons of my blouse and worked its way into my navel. The engraved scorpions were covered now, too. I envisioned them coming to life and tunneling toward us through the sand.

"*Matet*," Anubis said, reading from the new scroll case he'd retrieved. As he backtracked to the first relief, Sekhmet grabbed the case in my hand. She ripped open the seal and held it up to the light.

"This is *Tefen*." She thrust it back at me and pointed toward Anubis. "He's with the second Isis."

"I'll trade you for *Mestetef*," Anubis said, already having swapped cases again.

We reached back and forth, exchanging scroll cases with sweaty fingers until we were left with only two—the two that belonged to the hissing spouts currently burying us alive.

Playing musical scroll cases hadn't changed the fact that the room was still filling with sand, and there was nothing we could do about it.

We were going to die here.

Even my heart had surrendered to the idea, its racing fading to a sluggish beat. Or maybe that was just the weight of the sand cutting off circulation.

Bub stood up straighter and lifted his arms as the sand piled around his chest. Haunting blue light filled the remaining space in the chamber, lighting the creased faces of my tomb mates, including the seven faces of Isis, all that remained visible of her reliefs.

Sekhmet grunted and moved closer to the wall, pressing her ear between the two fonts. "Do you hear that?"

"Our impending death?" I asked. The goddess glared at me.

"No, reaper. The secondary trickling of sand from one vessel to another." She moved her head to a different spot. "I think one of these reservoirs feeds into the other."

"Then if we block one, the other might empty long enough to insert the scroll case?" Anubis asked, perking at the idea. He shoved the case he held at the first hole, spraying sand in our eyes without warning. I spat and turned my face away, blindly reaching up to help him hold the case steady.

At first, nothing happened. But then, the sand spilling from the other spout slowed to a trickle.

Sekhmet didn't wait for it to completely stop before cramming her case into the opening. It clicked, and the lapis lazuli flared to life, lending its blue light to the room and lightening our spirits. For a second, anyway.

"Perhaps…" Anubis began, licking his lips. "If the sand compacts at the top of the reservoir, we can clear out enough to insert this last one before it fills in again."

"We would need water for that," Sekhmet said.

"Or heat?" I suggested, considering the Latin fire spell I'd learned during the demonic training that had first put Bub in my path.

"No." Bub shook his head, knowing full well what I was proposing. "Sand melts into glass, love. It's too dangerous."

"Fire!" Sekhmet gasped. "Of course. My powers may be diminished on the mortal side, but within a temple dedicated to my mother form, I am not entirely without."

She used my shoulders to propel herself through the sand, yanking my hands away from the scroll case. Sand sprayed around the stone cap, but Sekhmet ignored Anubis's protests. Something in her face had shifted. Her nose flattened, and her upper lip curled back to meet it, exposing teeth that in no way resembled a human's.

Soon, Sekhmet's entire face was that of a lioness. The thick braids remained, though feline ears speared through her hair. She shimmied her shoulders, shaking the sand away from her neck where skin faded into fur.

I swallowed a yelp as Bub's hand found mine beneath the surface of the sand and squeezed. He tugged me away from Sekhmet, giving her a wider berth as she focused her attention on the hole above the lightless Isis. Anubis's brow pinched with uncertainty, but he let her push him and the scroll case aside. Confronting her in this form did not seem like a wise idea, even if we were literal inches from death.

Sand continued to spill in around us. It tickled my throat and filled in the hollows of my collarbones. I reminded myself to breathe, though there wasn't much air left in the room. Delirium was taking hold, and thoughts of death crept back in like circling sharks.

Bub's hand tightened around mine, drawing my attention. He gave me a pained look, then his gaze shot to our deity companions. Whatever parting words we shared would have to endure their audience.

"I'm so sorry I dragged you into this," I said, offering him a weak smile. "I love you."

"Yes, yes. You, too." His expression tightened. "Can you feel your feet?"

I wiggled my toes, not immediately understanding why he would ask such a thing, or how he could offer such lackluster sentiment in our final moments. I blamed the lack of oxygen.

Then I remembered Winston's skeleton coin in the heel of my left boot. If there was ever an emergency worthy of testing its ability, surely this was it. Bub blinked at me expectantly.

I sucked in a trembling breath and bent my knee, only managing to lift it an inch. The effort made my head swim, and my next rasping inhale included a fair amount of sand. I gagged and sputtered, but my hands were too heavy and too far away to clear the crust forming on my lips.

"Try again," Bub hissed, eyes swelling as the sand grazed his chin.

Before I had the chance, fire splashed across the wall of blue orbs.

Smoke curled around Sekhmet's feline nose. She pressed it against the stretch of stone above the sand spout as flames spewed from her pursed lips and into the hole. The falling sand turned to molten glass and dripped down the face of the engraved Isis below.

"Now!" Anubis thrust the scroll case at her, moving it across the surface of the sand as best he could with mostly buried arms.

Sekhmet pulled back from the hole, and together they shoved the case through the smoking goop. I twisted away as it splattered in my direction, the drops hissing as they hit the sand near my face.

My eyes squeezed shut, but I strained to listen through the roar of flame and sand and divine frustration—until the telltale *click* of the case sliding home unleashed a flood of endorphins.

When I turned back to the wall, the disks above Isis's seven heads all glowed a haunting blue, as if the suns had set and moons had risen in their place. Secrets bloomed best at night, after all.

"We did it!" Anubis howled out a giddy cackle. We were still buried up to our necks, but it was impossible not to appreciate the hard-won victory. Even if we could only bob our heads in celebration. Sekhmet's growl of laughter rattled through the chamber, but it soon dissolved into a more human sound as her face shifted again.

My body felt lighter, but it was more than just the relief. Something was happening. The hiss of sand continued to ring in my ears, though it was fainter. I'd assumed it was residual, like the blare of traffic horns that lingered after a day of harvesting souls in New York City.

But this sound was getting louder.

"The room is draining," Anubis said, lifting an arm above the surface. "Once it's cleared, perhaps the rotating door will work again."

"Lovely." Bub ran a hand over his face, clearing away sand that had stuck to his jaw. I wiggled my arms and managed to free a hand to clear my own face, though the sand in my mouth would need more help.

"I'd skin a hellcat for a drink of water right now," I groaned.

"Here." Sekhmet's hand emerged from the sand with a stainless-steel bottle that must have been hidden in the folds of her skirt. She gave it a shake, sloshing the contents inside. I eagerly accepted it before freeing my other arm to unscrew the cap.

"Hey!" Anubis frowned at her. "We could have used that to clump the sand."

Sekhmet snorted. "And waste perfectly good beer?"

I choked on my first mouthful. It wasn't just beer—it was *strong* beer. The foamy brew burned in my nose and made my eyes water.

"I'm okay," I rasped as Bub gripped my shoulder. I took another gulp, and then he cleared his throat.

"Don't be greedy, pet."

My face flushed as I handed over the bottle. Bub took a long drink before giving it back, but Sekhmet reclaimed the bottle before I could steal another sip. As she passed it to Anubis, the sand shifted, dropping several inches lower.

Another click sounded from the wall of hieroglyphs, and a circle of stone beneath a wing of the central Isis relief popped free. It dropped into the sand, revealing another lapis lazuli stone. It was smaller than the others, closer in size to a tangerine.

"Should we...?" I began, considering the risks more carefully this time.

"The riddle is solved, and the room is draining," Anubis said, pausing to take another drink before continuing. "I think this is our reward."

Sekhmet reached out first. She curled her fingers around the stone and tugged the case out of the wall. We all held our breaths, waiting to see if the new hole held any more surprises for us.

"I think we're safe." I sighed as the sand level dropped closer to my waist. It was easier to breathe, though my head still swam with relief and a tingling buzz from the beer.

"Here." Sekhmet handed the scroll case to me. "This is why you're here. You're the one who must open it."

I licked the corners of my mouth and turned the case over to find the wax seal. It was the same deep red as the others, thickly applied over the seam of the stiff leather.

"Go on," Sekhmet said, encouraging me.

I slipped a fingernail under the wax and broke it free.

There was no cavity inside this case. The leather un-wound like a roll of wrapping paper. Fixed to its other side was a papyrus scroll covered in more hieroglyphs, illustrations, and a map. I could tell it was of Egypt from the line of the Nile River leading up to the Mediterranean Sea.

The sand level dropped past my hips, and I wobbled unsteadily, trying to regain my balance as my vision blurred. Was the room spinning?

"Let me have a look." Sekhmet took the scroll from me, freeing my hands so I could use them to steady myself against the wall. My lungs were suddenly heavy again, and something was trying to icepick its way out of my skull.

Bub groaned beside me. He raked a hand through his hair and squeezed his head. "What was in that beer?"

Anubis threw the bottle at the goddess, but she swatted it away, laughing as he slumped in the sand. His eyelids sagged, even as he gritted his teeth. "Lady of Slaughter, have you no shame?"

"Such a good boy," she cooed. "But I warned you. We cat people are our own masters."

CHAPTER TWELVE

"The only cure for a real hangover is death."
—Robert Benchley

I WOKE WITH THE TASTE OF VOMIT in the back of my throat. The room reeked of it, and guttural retching echoed all around. I peeled my eyes open, immediately closing them against the harsh blue light spilling from the wall of orbs.

Sand stuck to my skin and sifted from my hair as I sat up. It covered the chamber floor, but not so completely that my back and hips didn't ache from the involuntary nap on a stone slab.

"Bub?" I whispered his name between uneven breaths, mindful of the nausea churning my insides. I didn't want to encourage it, but the panic wasn't helping either. "Beelzebub?" I called louder, blinking my eyes open again to find him slumped in the corner.

"I'm awake," he croaked. Then he made an awful noise that triggered my gag reflex.

The light in the room pulsed in time with my throbbing head, but I fought the urge to vomit until I'd dragged myself into the opposite corner. Bub's hand found the back of my neck, and he brushed the hair away from my sweaty nape as I threw up Sekhmet's tainted beer.

"Better out than in," he said, earning a grunt of agreement from Anubis.

When I finished, I used the wall to pull myself upright and moved toward the hidden door. The smell was unbearable, and though the room was cooler, I craved fresh air. I shoved my shoulder into the wall, wincing when it refused to budge.

"Look at the floor," Anubis said. He covered his mouth with one hand, not trusting the hiccup that followed, and used his other to point out the seam around the original wall that had folded inward. It was covered in sand. "There must be another way out," he said, turning back to the glowing orbs to scan the hieroglyphs for a solution.

"At least you can reach your boots now," Bub said under his breath.

"Let's not resort to that just yet." I rubbed my arm and considered the wall again, searching for a handhold or lever. "We're not in the same pickle as earlier."

"I'd like to know how much earlier." Bub held up his bare wrist. "My watch is missing. Along with my phone and coin," he added, patting his pockets. Mine were empty as well, and the daggers had been removed from my boots.

"Here we are." Anubis chanted something in a language I didn't recognize, and the hazy glow of the orbs focused into sharp rays. Their angles combined to form a singular beam that carved a line of white light on the opposite wall, beginning at the floor and tracing out a large rectangle that bled into a border of glowing symbols.

"Mother of the sun and moon, bring us forth into the light," Anubis said, opening his hand at the strange drawing as if it were a doorway. "Ladies first."

"Oh, hell no." I shook my head, stopping short when it throbbed out a warning. "If Sekhmet has any nasty surprises waiting for us, you get the first taste this time."

"As you wish." Anubis swallowed another hiccup, then stepped past me and through the wall. The surface of the stone quivered as if it were made of water, the pale light reflecting off its ripples. And then it was smooth again.

I hesitated, wondering if he'd come back or give us a signal of some sort. But then the symbols around the doorway flickered like a lightbulb just before it burns out.

The idea of being trapped in a puke-filled crypt propelled me forward. Bub latched onto my hand, and I pulled him through with me before dropping off the opposite side.

The surprise ripped a gasp from my raw throat. I'd expected to come out on the other side of the wall, in the mouth of the crypt. Instead, I caught a glimpse of blue sky. Then my knees buckled as my boots hit dirt. Bub landed more gracefully beside me, his steady hold keeping me from faceplanting.

A towering wall covered in hieroglyphs and giant reliefs loomed nearby. The defaced pillars were missing, but the size of the building and the surrounding landscape suggested this was the backside of Hathor's temple.

We were in the ruins of a much smaller chapel just a few yards away, though most of the outer wall was long gone. Luckily, the inner sanctuary remained intact. The doorway we'd come through was etched in stone on this side and elevated several feet off the ground. Clearly not for mortal use.

A handful of circular stone bases that had likely held statues of gods or pharaohs were spaced across the temple's foundation. Anubis rested on the nearest one, elbows folded over his knees as he squinted up at the sky. His white tunic shirt was wrinkled, and one khaki pant leg hadn't quite survived the second appearance of Sekhmet's beer.

"The temple will open soon," he said, blinking stiffly as he scratched the stubbled on his chin.

"No. That can't be right." I swallowed the bile tickling the back of my throat and turned to Bub, taking note of the growth along his jawline, too. But the thought of losing an entire day soon took a back seat. "The hounds!" I covered my face.

"I'm sure they've kept themselves entertained." Anubis's chuckle turned into a cough as I dropped my hands and glared at him.

"Yes," Bub grumbled. "I just hope they managed to safeguard our supplies while indulging in their debauchery."

My stomach gave another flop of dread when I considered the possibility of Sekhmet harming the hounds so she could steal our bags. Of course, she'd let *us* live. I hoped she'd extended the same courtesy to the dogs.

"Why didn't she just slit our throats?" I asked, following Anubis as he climbed over the remains of the chapel's wall. "She had plenty of time and opportunity."

"And desecrate the holy house of her mother form?" He shot a wide-eyed grimace over his shoulder at me. "Never. However bloodthirsty Sekhmet may be, she will never spill blood within these sacred walls, not even the portions dedicated to Isis," he added, nodding to a pair of large reliefs engraved among the hieroglyphs on the backside of the temple. "Isis as Cleopatra, alongside her mortal son, Cesarean," he detailed before pointing back to the ruins we'd just come from. "A fitting tribute adjacent to her birth house."

Bub caught my arm as I stumbled over the uneven stones placed around the temple. My head was still swimming, and my stomach knotted with uncertainty. I hoped both would subside once we found Saul and Coreen unharmed.

"What could Sekhmet want with the talisman?" Bub wondered aloud. "To restore Hathor, perhaps?"

"It's hard to say for certain." Anubis pointed out a large hole in the walkway as we cut around the side of the temple. "Careful there," he said, giving the hazard a wide berth. Once we were clear of it, he went on. "Many relics of Sekhmet's cult remain, though her following has not experienced the same renaissance as the Great Ennead and their children. She would need a mortal coven to bring Hathor into existence on this side."

He paused at a gated entrance into the temple and opened his hand, offering us entry ahead of him. I accepted this time, being able to see through the bars and screen, into the small chamber beyond.

My soul matter thinned, edging as close to the line between this world and the next as allowed without the aid of a coin, until I was able to slip through the locked gate. Bub followed, placing a hand on the small of my back. Once inside, we waited for Anubis to take the lead again. The temple was dark in the off-hours, and we had only a handful of tiny windows to light our way.

Soon we found ourselves in the open sky chapel again, staring down into the shadows of the crypt below. Before I could call for the hounds, Saul appeared at the foot of the ladder, ears perked and tail wagging. He whined, although the sound was somewhat muffled with the strap of my bag clenched in his jaws.

"Coreen?" I shouted, waiting for his sister to appear behind him looking guilty and sated. But she didn't. Neither did Anubis's jackals emerge from the shadows.

Saul whined again as Bub took his time climbing down the ladder. I imagined my demon's head and guts were in no condition for daring stunts. As soon as he stepped off the bottom rung, Saul dropped my bag and ran a circle around his legs, nearly knocking him over before bounding up the ladder and racing a few laps around me. I ruffled his ears and bent over to kiss the top of his nose, too grateful he was safe to care what Anubis thought of the display.

"The others are not down here," Bub called. "But there's no sign of a scuffle—or orgy, for that matter. And our supplies are relatively unharmed, albeit furry." He gave Saul a pointed scowl as he dusted off our hats.

"They probably went to find a quiet spot where they wouldn't be interrupted." I sighed and began a mental checklist of the supplies we were going to need for the mayhem that would soon follow.

"Perhaps they went for help?" Anubis suggested, then cackled at my skeptical glare. "Regardless, I'll be able to locate them through our summoning bond once we return to Duat."

"You can't do that now?" I asked before remembering both Bub's and Sekhmet's admissions about their lacking powers on the mortal side. "Oh. Right."

Anubis smiled apologetically. "I'm sure Coreen is with them, and you'll be reunited soon."

I didn't doubt it. Besides, we had bigger problems to deal with right now. What we were going to do with another litter of helljack puppies was a question for another day.

"I'll have a talk with Hades," Bub said. "If we give the pups to him, perhaps he'll finally agree to spay the little tart." He tossed my hat up from the crypt, and I caught it with a wince.

My aching skull was not a fan of sudden moves. Dehydration was at least half to blame. Hopefully a drink would ease my suffering.

Bub dug a canteen out of his bag and took a few careful swallows before handing it up to me. I was so ready to get the taste of vomit and sand out of my mouth, I would have eaten an entire tube of toothpaste.

The cool water rocked a shiver through my shoulders, and my stomach gurgled. I couldn't decide if it was in warning or relief, but I continued guzzling, stopping just shy of draining the canteen when I caught Anubis staring.

"Sorry." Heat flooded my face as I offered him a drink. "There's more in my bag," I said as the last of the canteen dripped into his open mouth.

"And we have a few backup bottles," Bub added. "Hopefully that will be enough to get us to the nearest hospital."

"Hospital?" Anubis frowned as he accepted the second canteen from Bub and offered his free hand to help my demon up the last few steps of the ladder with our bags in tow.

"That's the best place to run into a reaper and hitch a ride home, yes?"

"Well, sure," Anubis conceded, pausing to take a long drink from the canteen. "I just didn't figure you'd throw in the towel so easily."

Bub gave him a puzzled frown. "What more can we do here?"

"We know where Sekhmet's going," Anubis said. "She's already gotten a day's head start on us, and with coin to travel on at that."

"Yes, but…" Bub huffed and slung a bag over his shoulder. "Don't you think we should report this turn of events to Isis? Besides, we're rather useless on this side without coin."

He had a point. My hand involuntarily went to my pocket, searching again for all that Sekhmet had pilfered. The skeleton coin in my boot was the only thing keeping me from having a meltdown, but I was willing to give Bub's plan a go first.

Anubis sighed and cocked his head at the exit. "The hospital is across the river. It's on the way to the train station, so I'll drop you off there."

"You're going to ride the train to Alexandria? Won't that take all day?" I accepted the canteen from him, tilting it down to drizzle some water out for Saul. My hound lapped at the stream, splashing slobber in all directions. "Wouldn't it be faster to come with us and then return by coin?" I asked.

"Maybe." Anubis shrugged. "Or maybe you'll end up waiting at the hospital for a few days before a reaper drops in. Who knows? And I'm taking the train to Cairo. I have a stash of coins at a museum there."

"Is that so?" I said, noticing Anubis's sly grin as he turned to lead us out of the chapel. I took my bag from Bub and made a face. "He could be right about the hospital wait time."

Bub grumbled under his breath, but he let the unspoken question hang in the air between us as we followed Anubis through the temple, past the Hathor-headed columns and into the courtyard. The sound of light traffic hummed in the distance as we made our way toward the gated pylon.

The headache I'd woken with had faded to the background, but I felt it creeping in again. It throbbed with every step I took, intensifying as the sun rose higher in the sky. The palm trees offered little shade, and soon we were surrounded by farmland.

Anubis cut right, turning onto a road between two fields of sugarcane. "This is a shortcut to the bridge," he said. "It's only a few kilometers from here."

"Super." I sucked in a deep breath and wrapped both hands around the strap of my bag. If I could make it that far without dropping dead, I was sure I could convince Bub to hop a train to Cairo.

Anubis needed a reaper to harvest the talisman, after all. If I called it quits, I was sure the second he had a coin in hand, he'd fetch Tasha to complete the job. I wasn't about to let that happen. I owed Sekhmet an ass-kicking anyway. This was a two-birds-one-stone mission now.

I gritted my teeth and marched past the stabbing in my brain. Saul trotted along beside me, occasionally licking my elbow for moral support, while Bub kept pace with Anubis up ahead. He glanced over his shoulder a time or two, but I met his concern with a strained smile. A little walk through the countryside would not be the end of me. Not today, Satan.

The sound of traffic returned as we neared the next intersection, and Anubis directed us onto the sidewalk of a busy road. Shops and restaurants crowded together, displaying colorful signs in Arabic. The smell of coffee mixed with exhaust and something sickly sweet pushed a lump up the back of my throat. Before I knew what had hit me, I was hunched over the curb, retching.

Bub rubbed my back. Saul was less helpful, standing directly in front of me as if prepared to attack whatever invisible force was giving me a hard time.

"I'm fine," I rasped. "Just give me a second—and give *him* a treat so he'll get out of the splash zone."

Bub clicked his tongue and rested his bag on the hood of a nearby car. The sound of the zipper did the trick and lured Saul away. I was grateful the few locals loitering about couldn't see me.

Anubis wandered half a block ahead, offering a bit more privacy. He reclined against a soda delivery truck while the driver carried on a conversation with a waiter in front of a nearby café. When I'd finally composed myself and Saul had finished horking down his snack, the god returned with a skip in his step.

"There was a fire at a bottling facility in Cairo," he announced with a little too much glee.

"That's… nice." I wiped my mouth with the back of my hand and accepted a bottle of water from Bub. "How many dead?"

"None." Anubis hiked a thumb behind him toward the delivery truck. "But they don't have enough product for some event at the pyramids tonight, so that driver is making a special trip."

"You want us to ride in the back of a soda truck to Cairo?" Bub scoffed. "You must be joking."

"It will shave two hours off the trip," Anubis said.

The café owner stepped out onto the sidewalk and shouted something at the waiter, spurring the driver to drag his loaded dolly inside. Anubis inched a step backward, likely sensing the window of opportunity was about to close.

"If you'd rather wait at the hospital, it's a few more kilometers that way," he said, pointing down the busy road. "You should see signs for it after crossing the bridge. Best of luck," he added as the driver appeared again. The man pushed his empty dolly up the ramp and into the cargo area, muttering under his breath the whole time. Anubis tossed us a short wave and hurried after him.

"I don't read Arabic." I turned to Bub. "Do you?"

The skin between his brows puckered, which was answer enough.

We both took off for the truck. Saul bounded after us, a dopey grin on his face at the promise of a new adventure.

CHAPTER THIRTEEN

"Never lose an opportunity of seeing anything beautiful,
for beauty is God's handwriting."
—Ralph Waldo Emerson

I COULDN'T IMAGINE THERE WERE MANY goddesses willing to ride seven hours in the back of a soda truck to secure their title—especially not with a hangover and a hellhound that had no concept of personal space.

The truck braked suddenly, and Saul rolled over my leg, his enormous head flopping in my lap. Doggy breath hit me square in the face, and I gagged as I fanned the stench away with my hat.

"Are we there yet?" I groaned. "My everything hurts."

The vehicle's lack of suspension made every dip and bump in the road feel like an amusement park ride gone wrong, and the lingering nausea and stifling heat made me ache with regret.

So much regret.

"We should have taken the train." Bub sighed and readjusted his backpack behind his head.

We'd been taking turns grumbling the same complaints since the ride began—however long ago that had been. Without a phone or watch, it was hard telling just how many hours we'd been cooped up between the stacked pallets.

"Still better than camels," Anubis chirped. He'd rearranged a few cases of soda to create his own little carbonated throne, and he looked entirely too comfortable. "And camels would have taken at least two weeks," he added, using his fingers to calculate some equation. "Finding this transport was a lucky coincidence."

"Yeah, lucky." I tilted my head back onto a pallet and tried to breathe through my nose.

Saul felt like a furnace pressed against my leg, but letting him remain was better than the steamroller treatment any time the truck turned or stopped suddenly.

The treats Bub had packed for the hounds were gone, but there were plenty of protein bars. None of us were brave enough to risk one yet. Not in such a confined space, anyway. Though we had split another bottle of water. It wasn't much, but it was best to ration our supply until we made it to Anubis's museum stash.

The mountains of soda all around us were useless. Sure, we could crack open a can or two and make one hell of a mess, but we couldn't drink it.

Long-term survival on the mortal side was tricky. There were stoups of holy water in churches considered potable to angels and saints. Deities could partake from sacred pools and springs in their native lands. Reapers could fortunately drink from any of the spiritual fonts. Demons had fewer options, but fresh, natural sources like rain—long-rooted in religious ceremonies—were fair game for all.

I'd spent an embarrassing amount of time in the back of the soda truck trying to convince myself that it might rain in Cairo. March was a little late in the season, but it wasn't impossible. Several years ago, the city had even experienced snow for the first time in over a hundred years. Of course, that had been in December.

I closed my eyes and sent up a prayer to whoever might be listening, begging for a similar miracle to be waiting for us when we arrived. I tried to imagine what drops of rain would feel like on my face and my tongue. Maybe I'd dissolve like a sand sculpture. I certainly felt as gritty as one.

Saul's head bounced in my lap as the truck slowed and turned onto another road. It turned again soon after, cuing Bub to sit up straight.

"Is it time for gas again so soon?" he pondered aloud. It felt too hopeful to assume our journey had come to an end.

Anubis stood and stretched his arms over his head. "I'll have a looksee as soon as we've stopped."

"We'll come with you," I said, nudging Saul aside. "I need some fresh air, and I think this one could use a potty break." Saul's ears perked, and he let out an affirmative bark.

"Just make it quick," Anubis warned. "Even if we've reached the pyramids, the museum is a good fifteen to twenty kilometers away. If the driver is staying overnight or checking in with the local warehouse, he'll likely be heading that way, and we can shorten the distance."

I nodded. "Sounds like a plan."

I mean, the idea of spending more time in the back of a truck didn't sound like a *great* plan, but it beat the hell out of walking for hours through a busy city to get where we were going.

The sliding back door of the truck rolled up, and daylight spilled inside. Despite my complete lack of surprise, I was disappointed it wasn't raining. I squinted, straining to see as my eyes adjusted, but was only rewarded with a narrow view of an alley. Someone shouted at the driver, and he replied in kind. I couldn't understand, but the man's brow flattened as he reached for the dolly in the corner. I gathered up my bag and eased a step back from the pallets nearest the door.

Anubis listened quietly, then relayed the situation to Bub and me as if he were explaining an Italian opera.

"The restaurant next door is completely sold out. They think their delivery should come first and that the driver is an idiot for serving a smaller business ahead of them. The driver is now threatening to take product to a lounge on the other side of the necropolis before returning with their order."

"So we have a bit of time?" Bub asked, poking his head out of the truck to have a better look around.

"Just a bit." Anubis tapped his chin thoughtfully. "I'd say our guy is bluffing, and his last stop will probably be at the lounge on the other side. It's a twenty-minute walk from here—a better use of our time than playing keep away from our unwitting friend, Big-Rig Ali," he said, squeezing between two stacks of pallets as the driver joined us to reload his two-wheeler.

As soon as the driver was gone, Bub threw his bag over one shoulder. "Fancy a stroll through the pyramids, love?" he asked as if we were carefree mortals on vacation.

I was in no mood for touristy sightseeing, but if it meant fresh air and a break from roasting in the metal box, I would have agreed to walk through a minefield.

I pressed my hat down on top of my head and slung the strap of my bag over my shoulder. Saul took the cue and jumped to his feet, tail thumping out a metallic rhythm on the inside wall of the truck. Maybe a little walk would do us all some good.

I gave Bub my hand and turned to Anubis. "Lead the way."

We cleared the ramp just as the driver reappeared. The street was narrow but featured bright, clean sidewalks. Lush trees reached over low garden walls. It was a peculiar sight considering how close we were to the desert. We'd no more than circled the delivery truck and I could already see the pyramids cutting into the skyline.

The modern world was constantly encroaching on the ancient, but I still found the contrast jarring. Even more alarming was the sheer size of the monuments. I'd known they were big, but to see them in comparison to the surrounding city was humbling.

Anubis paused beneath a nearby tree, and we waited to make sure the driver wouldn't make good on his threat to reroute his deliveries out of spite. If he did, my vote was for relaxing at the snooty restaurant until he returned. When he wheeled his next load toward the opposite side of the street, we carried on.

Half a block later, the Sphinx came into view, and then the shops and restaurants gave way to sand. Camels lounged beside a road that cut between the two largest pyramids up ahead, and several horse carts and buses ventured our way, hauling tourists toward the exit.

"It's almost closing time," Anubis explained before pointing south, past the sphinx and pyramids, to a structure perched atop a sandy ridge in the distance. "That's our destination."

I made a face at the uneven landscape and then gazed longingly up the smooth road that curled around the pyramids. Desert treks were nothing new for me—Bub and I enjoyed regular runs with the hounds on the desert trail behind the manor in Tartarus—but with the toxic beer hangover and bumpy truck ride, I just wasn't feeling it.

"We'll make our way behind the Sphinx and through the mastabas," Anubis said, leaning over the block wall surrounding the monument.

More excavation was underway, unearthing the bottom half of the Sphinx that had spent much of recent history under the sand. The drop behind the wall was less severe farther up the road. Anubis waved us along, but only Saul trotted after him with any enthusiasm.

"Last of the seven wonders, and we don't even have a phone for the customary selfie. Tragic," Bub said, his gaze lingering on the pyramids we wouldn't have time to explore. "We should come back here sometime. When we're not in survival mode, obviously."

"Yeah." I sighed. A real vacation sounded nice. But a vacation in Eternity, where Bub's swarm of flies could carry me about as if they were a magic carpet, sounded even better. A whole new world, indeed.

"Here we go." Anubis slapped a spot on the wall. Then he braced one hand on the rounded blocks along the top and leapt over. Saul went next, his giant paws tossing up sand as he touched down beside Anubis. Bub, ever the gentleman, offered me his hand.

"I'll manage, Prince Charming," I said with a grin. He shrugged and climbed over the wall with more care than Anubis had, mindful of the supplies strapped to his back. Busted water bottles would have been a crime at this point.

I slid my bag off my shoulder, deciding I'd toss it down before making the jump. But I never got the chance.

A foot planted in the center of my back. I lurched forward, pulling the bag up to keep from eating the block wall, though the air was knocked from my lungs. Before I could suck in a breath, my legs were swept out from under me, and I was hurled into the air.

I caught a flash of red fabric as the world turned upside down.

CHAPTER FOURTEEN

"If you don't die of thirst, there are blessings in the desert."
—Anne Lamott

WITH A DEMON, A GOD, AND A HELLHOUND waiting below, I had expected *someone* would break my fall. I'd also mistakenly assumed the sand would soften the blow of my graceless landing. Or at least let me off without a concussion.

As I waited for the world to stop spinning, Bub and Anubis stared down at me, brows pinched with concern and mouths moving. But I couldn't hear them over the ringing in my ears.

"*Bitch,*" I whispered, still struggling to find the air that had been forcefully ejected from my lungs.

Anubis frowned and stood upright. "That was uncalled for," he said, the words sounding fuzzy and distant as my hearing returned.

"I tried to help you." Bub squatted beside me and took the bag gripped in my hands. It hadn't done much good on the way down, but I could at least be grateful the water bottle inside had survived.

"Sekhmet," I rasped. "She's here."

"You're certain?" Anubis's gaze snapped up in time for him to watch the goddess soar over the wall. Her red skirt billowed around her waist as she delivered a kick to the center of his chest. He grunted in surprise but grabbed hold of her ankle before she could get away.

Sekhmet let out a squeal as he twisted sideways and slammed her into the ground next to me. She recovered quickly, rolling out of the path of Anubis's sandaled foot before it stamped right where her head had been.

"Idiots," she hissed, scrambling to her feet. "You should have quit when you had the chance. I've no qualms about killing you here."

"Oh yeah?" I grunted and pulled myself up onto an elbow. "Well, I don't have a problem killing *you* any-where."

My hands itched to wrap around her neck and wring it, but then I spotted the leather case strapped to her hip. Bub noticed, too. He made a grab for it, but Sekhmet was faster. Her leg whipped up sharply, and she spun a tight circle before bringing her heel down across the back of Bub's skull.

His face smashed into the sand at my feet, and his arms flopped uselessly over my calves, pinning me to the ground. Saul let out a confused yap at the display as if he weren't sure whether he should intervene. To be fair, he'd witnessed plenty of sparring sessions with my apprentices in the backyard, and the last time he'd seen Sekhmet, we'd all been playing nice.

"*Appugno!*" I shouted, pointing at the goddess. Her eyes swelled at the Latin command, and she tore off across the desert with Saul bounding after her.

Anubis looked like he might give chase as well, but then a distant yowl drew his attention back to the wall. I knew that sound.

"Are you okay?" I tugged at Bub's arm, trying to maintain patience as my panic bloomed.

"I think so." He touched his head and winced. I gave his other arm a yank to free my legs.

"Good, then get up," I said, pulling him along with me as I stood. "We're gonna have to make a run for it."

Bub blinked stiffly, but then the sound came again. It was louder—or closer. I couldn't quite tell. When a third yowl split the air before the second had finished, I nearly swallowed my tongue. There was more than one of them.

Anubis's nostrils flared, and he sucked in a startled breath. "Hellcats."

"Did Sekhmet summon them?" I whispered. "Can she *do* that?"

"I don't know," he admitted. "She is a cat goddess, and we are at a sacred site with an iconic feline monument." He waved a hand at the backside of the Sphinx. "I guess it's possible."

"We have no weapons, and our powers are diminished," Bub said, outlining our obvious predicament. Well, *their* predicament, anyway.

"My powers work just fine." I flexed my fingers, wondering how much damage a hellcat could do before I pulled its soul matter inside out. If all else failed, maybe that Latin fire spell would come in handy after all. "I'll distract them while you two go after Sekhmet."

"Not a chance." Bub scowled at me. "I'm not leaving you here to fend off hellcats by yourself."

"What are you going to do? Throw sand in their eyes?" I stretched an arm across my chest, trying to loosen the aching muscles in my back. "We *need* that scroll," I said. "I think you can handle that while I take care of these strays."

"This is a terrible idea." He touched his head again and gritted his teeth. "Are you sure?"

"As sure as anyone can be about wrangling feral creatures from hell." I glanced up at the sky, then eased onto my toes and peeked over the wall, scanning the stretch of street on the other side.

Nothing.

I would have been more relieved if I hadn't known how fast the creatures could travel. I knew what kind of damage they were capable of, too. They'd all but sunk my ship on more than one occasion.

"Didn't you pack some rope?" I asked Bub.

His frown deepened. "This is no time for John Wayne antics."

"I can't think of a better time." I wondered how the Duke would have fared in *Hatari!* with the monsters we were up against. His Jeep had survived a rhinoceros, but I had a feeling hellcats would have called for a tank. I had neither.

"Who's John Wayne?" Anubis asked. "A beastly deity?"

"Only on the silver screen." Bub snorted.

"Just give me the rope." I held out my hand, shaking it to hurry him when the hellcats started in again, this time screeching back and forth. It was the sort of racket meant to startle prey into running out into the open, and while it made my skin crawl, it also confirmed their numbers. "There are only two of them."

"*Only* two." Bub scoffed, but he unzipped his pack and began digging through his supplies. "Terrible, terrible idea," he grumbled under his breath.

I hitched a brow at him. "Do you have a better one?"

"As a matter of fact…" His gaze dropped to my boot, but I snatched the rope from him before he could mention the skeleton coin.

"I'll be fine," I insisted. "Just get the scroll. Can you do that?"

"We'll do our best." Anubis scooped up my bag and slung it across his back. "Let's hope your hound takes some of the fight out of Sekhmet before we catch up."

I stared out across the desert, searching for them, but the trail ended near the scattered rock tombs beyond the Sphinx. Maybe Saul had cornered her in one. At the very least, the tombs would offer some cover while I tried to wrangle the cats.

"I'll draw them away—give them a run around the pyramids while you gain some ground," I said, bending down to take a closer look at the rope.

I didn't know much about lassos, but I'd been sailing the Sea of Eternity for a few centuries, so I wasn't entirely clueless when it came to knots. I tied a running bowline, creating a noose at one end of the rope. The limp nylon didn't make for a picture-perfect lasso, but I hoped it would get the job done.

"I still don't like this." Bub sighed, but he leaned over and pressed a kiss to my forehead. "I'll be very cross if you get eaten."

"And I'll be eternally humiliated," Anubis added. "Horus will never let me live it down."

Bub huffed. "He's the one who recommended Lana. If anything happens to her, I'll take my vengeance on him first."

"I'm sure." I grinned and wrapped a hand behind Bub's neck to pull him back down for a real kiss.

"I'm serious," he said. "Armageddon will seem a cheerful holiday against my grieving warpath."

"I believe you. Now get ready. I'm about to trade this frying pan for the fire."

Bub resecured his pack and moved farther down the wall to stand near Anubis. I waited until they were lined up with a clear shot to the tombs before standing and taking another look around.

My chest ached with each breath, though I couldn't tell if it was from anxiety or the bone-crunching drop over the wall. The rope felt soft and useless in my hands, and I desperately wished it was my axe instead. I would have even settled for one of Warren's shoddy retractable scythes and a can of angelica mace. What the hell was I going to do with a hellcat if I did manage to hogtie the damn thing?

It had been years since I'd last cast the fire spell, and longer still since I'd used my grim ability to undo a being's soul matter. What if I couldn't pull it off?

The shriek of a hellcat put my doubts on the backburner, and I jolted away from the wall, tearing across the desert toward the nearest pyramid. My pulse trembled in my throat, and I remembered to breathe— immediately forgetting again when the first cat appeared.

The hideous creature looked less like a cat and more like a dead horse whose skin had baked to its skeleton. It scaled the base of the pyramid, navigating the massive stones with its taloned toes, leather wings folded in against its bony spine. The sun hung low in the western sky. It painted shadows on the visible side of the monument, almost camouflaging the creature's dark hide. If it hadn't moved, I might not have noticed it at all.

The sound of wings beating the air drew my focus to the next pyramid over in time to watch the second hellcat take flight. Its smoldering eyes locked onto mine, and it shrieked a warning to its companion.

Who knew hellcats had enough brains for teamwork? *Not me.*

CHAPTER FIFTEEN

"What doesn't kill you makes you stronger.
Except cowgirls. Cowgirls will kill you."
—Ray Cole

"Shit. shit. shit," I chanted under my breath, still racing toward certain doom like a maniac with a death wish. I tried to invoke John Wayne and whipped the looped end of the rope in the air, preparing to do something. Not that I knew what that something would be.

I just needed to buy the guys enough time to get to the tombs. Then I could run like hell, or finally take the skeleton coin for a test ride like Bub kept suggesting.

The hellcat on the pyramid screeched out a hateful greeting as I neared. I waited for it to leap down to meet me head on. When it didn't, I let common sense—and terror—detour me around the south side of the structure, in the opposite direction of the airborne cat.

Of course, there was no winning a footrace against demonic beasts. Certainly not against one that had taken to the sky.

The creature dropped in my path. Its enormous wings swept sand and rocks into my face, but it was the guttural hiss through an arsenal of rotting, broken teeth that put the brakes on for me. Breath like raw sewage drifted across the void, turning my stomach, but I widened my stance, planting my boots firmly as I loosened the loop of my makeshift lasso. I didn't expect it to hold up long against the hellcat's claws, but if I could tangle it up even for a moment, maybe I could take shelter in the pyramid before it caught up with me again.

A low growl pulled my attention back to the first cat. I was surprised it hadn't taken to the air, but when it shook out its wings, I understood why. This wasn't its first rodeo.

The leathery webbing was torn through, likely by the blade of a reaper's scythe or a Nephilim Guard's spear. There had been numerous sightings last winter before I'd been commissioned to help seal up the breached boundaries of various underworlds. Stragglers were inevitable.

Before I could be grateful for the beast's handicap, its partner rushed me. I threw the loop without thinking and rolled out of the hellcat's path. As soon as I regained my footing, I gave the rope a tug and whooped at the resistance. Until I was jerked off my feet again.

My hat blew free as my face smashed against the ground. I came away with a mouthful of sand. It found its way into my eyes and nose, as well. I sputtered and blinked up at the beast, squinting to see what I'd caught.

One leathery wing cut through the air, yanking the rope and me along with each thrust. The lasso had caught around the base of the appendage where the bone connected to the hellcat's spine. It coiled tighter, pinching in the other wing as the cat spun in circles, blindly swiping its claws. I wrapped the rope around my forearm and held it taut to keep it out of the creature's reach. The tactic won me another mouthful of sand as I was dragged across the desert floor.

The second hellcat crept closer as if to aid its demonic kin, but a trapped cat trusts no one. Least of all a creature that was just as likely to eat it as hump it. Still, if I didn't make a move soon, I was going to run out of rope, and time.

I waited for the beast to twist one more circle, further tangling its wings. Then I scraped together the nerve to drag myself to my feet and leapt onto the beast's hind quarters. I resisted the urge to whoop this time, saving my breath for the bucking ride of my life. My teeth rattled in my skull, and every joint and muscle in my body tightened until I was little more than a rubber band on the verge of snapping.

When the bucking failed to shake me loose, the hellcat snarled and lifted a back leg, blindly slashing its open claws at my ankles. But I had the high ground now. I stomped a heel into its bony ass, and it took off like a shot.

The beast's leathery wings slapped at my arms and face, but I held firm, gritting my teeth against the ache building in my wrist where the rope was cutting off circulation. My eyes watered in the wind, but I squinted ahead, scanning the dunes for more foes.

Instead, I spotted my misfit crew. Saul had caught up with Sekhmet in the open stretch of desert near the smallest of the three pyramids. One end of the scroll case was gripped in his teeth, the other clutched in Sekhmet's hands in a deadly game of tug-of-war. Anubis and Bub weren't far behind and closing in quickly. They'd have the scroll any second now. Only I was about to crash the party with an angry hellcat, and I hadn't even the courtesy to muzzle it first. How rude of me.

I glanced down at my unwilling steed's torso as if I might find an emergency brake. No such luck. I considered the fire spell, but if dropping a hellcat in the mix was a bad idea, I couldn't see how a *flaming* hellcat would be any better.

If my soul-sucking trick still worked, it was now or never.

I looped the rope around my elbow, trying to relieve my wrist before freeing my other hand. My feet felt unsteady, the soles of my boots slipping against the cat's slick body as the beast worked up a sweat. I flexed my fingers and tried to recall what had triggered my grim ability. How could I recreate it?

There had been Craig Hogan, who'd brought me very near to death before I discovered I could pull his wretched heart right out of his chest and erase him from the history books. And then Grim, who had killed nearly everyone I loved before my grief had swallowed him whole.

But I really didn't want to toe either of those lines, and I couldn't exactly recreate them with only a second's notice. There had to be another way.

Before I could think on it any further, Sekhmet kicked Saul in the ribs. He released the scroll and yelped. The sound boiled in my guts, hot as cheap tequila, and then it spread to my palm—the same way it had when I found out Maalik had killed my mentor.

Wrath. Of course.

I was like the Hulk, if the Hulk ate souls when someone made him angry instead of smashing. Though I would have much rather visualized the angel's stupid face than watch a cutthroat goddess abuse my hound.

With the hellcat's frantic pace, it took all my effort to squat on its back. The strain on the rope only seemed to increase its speed, but I cupped my palm around the thick ridge of its spine and pressed in until its soul matter caved.

The heat in my palm increased as something thick and oily wove through my fingers. I swallowed the bile rising in my throat and tried to steady my breath, pacing it in time with the creature's gallop. This would require careful timing.

I began to pull, and the cat trembled around my submerged hand. I prayed it wouldn't stop to test its back claws on me again. My position was too vulnerable now, especially without knowing how much force it would take to undo a beast of this size.

Up ahead, Anubis had taken Saul's place. His knuckles turned white as he attempted to wrench the scroll case out of Sekhmet's grip. Bub took off his backpack and slugged the goddess in the side of the head, earning a squeal of annoyance from her. Saul circled them all, looking for a good place to jump in. I was currently doing the same. Just in case the hellcat didn't give up the ghost before we closed the distance. I was rusty, after all, and my confidence was waning.

The oily, tarry soul matter of the cat would not let go.

I strained against it, pulling with the rope and pushing with my feet. It felt as if my shoulder would pop out of its socket any second, but I couldn't stop. Mostly because I didn't want the thing to take a bite out of my consort, but also because I was about to piss myself from panic.

My hand was *stuck* in the back of a hellcat, and I couldn't get free.

A few seconds later, the hysteria took over, and I screamed. The sound reached the others, and suddenly all eyes were on me. I might have been embarrassed if I hadn't been so horrified.

My outburst startled the hellcat, too. It bucked its back legs, trying once again to shake me loose. Thankfully, it worked this time. Even better, I got to keep my hand.

The cat's dark soul matter unraveled like a broken Chinese finger trap. I rolled between the beast's wings, bringing the tendrils of its existence down in a ribbon-esque arc of smoke behind me as I collided with Sekhmet.

The scroll case sprang free, shooting up into the air where the hellcat's soul matter was quickly dispersing like exhaust from a diesel truck. It prompted a cheer from Bub. Anubis blinked up at the sky, having been knocked on his ass when I arrived on the scene. At least I'd stuck the landing.

Sekhmet thrashed beneath me, her eyes swollen with surprise and fear.

"Tag, you're it," I rasped in her face. I pressed my elbow into her breastbone, and she grunted out a pained snarl. A more ferocious sound echoed her as the other hellcat caught up.

"The scroll!" Anubis shouted. He reached for it, pulling his arm back just shy of having it bitten off. The beast snatched up the case in its jaws and chomped down, shredding the leather.

"No!" Without thinking, I threw my hand out. "*Sanctus Incendia!*"

The flames hit the hellcat in the throat and spread, lighting it up as if it were coated in napalm. Unfortunately, the scroll case caught fire, too. Bub kicked sand over it, which was the safer, saner option until the burning hellcat stopped shrieking and dropped dead.

The ear-splitting racket grated on my every nerve, but it was the smoldering scroll case that sucker-punched any sense of victory to be had. And my sulking disappointment was all the distraction Sekhmet needed. She twisted her hips suddenly, tossing me in the sand as she sprang to her feet.

"You fools!" she snarled, holding up a coin for us to see that she'd secured her escape. "I've already studied the scroll, and you're still trapped on mortal land. What can you possibly hope to accomplish?"

She didn't wait for an answer before rolling the coin and vanishing, leaving us alone in the desert with a smoking hellcat corpse as the sun set behind the pyramids.

"Hey... Hey!" Anubis pointed.

I twisted around, expecting to find Sekhmet creeping up behind me. Instead, I spotted the lounge on the horizon—and a soda truck pulling away from the entrance.

"Gah!" Anubis squeezed his head with both hands and groaned. "There goes our ride."

I sighed and glanced down at my raw wrist and blistered palm. My shoulder was in rough shape, too. I wasn't looking forward to the rest of the injury assessment, but it was put on hold as the sound of wet gnawing came from the stinking carcass.

Saul buried his muzzle in the creature's charred belly. He glanced up at my grunt of disgust and licked the blood from his nose, innocently cocking his big dumb head.

Bub had a different reaction. His forked tongue flicked the corners of his mouth. "Is anyone else hungry?"

My stomach made a questionable noise as I redirected my disgust. "I'm not *that* hungry."

"I meant the protein bars, pet." He held up his backpack and gave it a shake, though I didn't miss the smirk he tried to hide.

"I'd rather have a drink of water," I confessed.

"Me, too," Anubis said. "There are water tunnels deep beneath the pyramids, once thought to be linked to Duat. As a fixture of the Egyptian underworld, I have access. I'll refill the canteens."

"Super." I looked back at the scroll, still half-buried in sand and smoking. I was fresh out of optimism, but that wouldn't stop me from having a peek at what was left. Anything was better than nothing, but I'd made do with less.

CHAPTER SIXTEEN

THERE WAS A SHELTER BUILT OVER the lower entrance of the central pyramid—Khafre's pyramid, Anubis had explained before leaving Bub and me to wait on one of the wooden benches while he went to refill our canteens. It was a good spot that I'd missed during the hellcat rodeo, seeing as how it was on the north side of the pyramid. If any more hellcats appeared to eat our faces off, we'd have plenty of time to take cover in the tunnel below. At least, that's what I told myself as I did my damnedest to focus on the remains of the scroll.

Between being treated like a chew toy and taking the brunt of my Latin blowtorch, Sekhmet's leather case was toast. As soon as it had cooled down enough to handle, we'd peeled it apart to reveal the scroll within. The seal had melted, and dark wax coated the seam of the tube's withered, leather backing. Some had soaked through, staining the portion of the document that had survived. I attributed that small mercy to the carnelian and lapis lazuli caps that held the scroll's shape, preventing it from contracting and shriveling in on itself. The stones were covered in soot, but they'd served a higher purpose than beauty today.

I held the charred scrap of papyrus up to the fading daylight and squinted at what I assumed was a partial map of Taposiris Magna. The rolled bandage Bub had been attempting to secure around my blistered hand dangled haphazardly from my wrist.

"Hold still," he griped, untangling the fabric so he could continue wrapping, taking the dressing up past my rope-burned wrist and nearly to my elbow. He finally stopped when I cleared my throat.

"Since when do you have a mummy fetish?" I asked, brows rising with concern.

"Sorry! Sorry." He sighed and trimmed the bandage before tucking the roll back into his bag. "I'm just… distracted. This little adventure has taken one too many wrong turns."

"We'll all feel better once we make it to the museum," I said, turning my gaze back to the scroll. "Does this mark here look like a scorpion?" I pointed out a smudged symbol on the page. "I sure hope we don't have to solve another puzzle to find this tomb." My nose scrunched at the idea of being buried alive again.

"Seriously?" Bub leaned away from me with a bewildered scowl. "After everything we've been through, don't you think it's time to cut our losses and go home?"

"After everything we've been through, are you really so eager to give up?" I countered. "Don't you *want* to be my consort?"

"Of course I do, but—" His jaw flexed, and he paused to rake a hand through his hair, taking a deep breath before going on. "We're ill-prepared, without weapons or our otherworldly abilities."

"Speak for yourself," I said, immediately regretting the comeback. "Once we reach Anubis's coin stash, we'll be able to hop over to the manor and weapon-up before hitting Taposiris. If Kevin and Eliza are back from Summerland, we'll bring them along as backup. I bet Anubis can wrestle up a friend or two, as well."

"That's a tidy plan." He gave me a patronizing frown. "A lot like every other plan we've had on this excursion, all of which have gone sideways."

I sighed and rolled my eyes, choosing to gaze out across the desert rather than at my broody demon. A dark shadow moved across the sand. My stomach flopped anxiously until I realized it was only Saul. He had the hellcat carcass in tow, dragging it along behind him by one of its mangled legs.

"That's close enough!" I shouted. The smell of charred flesh still clung to my clothes, but I'd choked down one of the protein bars at Bub's insistence.

Saul dropped the hellcat leg and wagged his tail as if he expected an attaboy for trying to share his meal with us.

"It's all yours, old sport," Bub said, sounding disappointed. I didn't suppose a demon took issue with eating any kind of meat, but he was considerate of my aversions. He knew what turned me off, and breath that reeked of sulfuric roadkill was near the top of the list. Though if we'd been out of protein bars, even I might have reevaluated our dinner options.

"Miss me?" Anubis called as he emerged from the underground stairwell. He held a dripping canteen in each hand. His clothes and hair were wet, too, but he didn't seem to mind. "It's a great day to be a god," he said, handing over the canteens before turning his wide smile toward the streak of golden light on the horizon.

I unscrewed the cap of my canteen and chugged the water, ignoring the headache brought on by its icy coldness. It was worth it. When I finished, Anubis disappeared long enough to refill it one more time. Then I tucked it away in my bag, hoping it would be enough for the rest of our trip.

Bub packed the second canteen and sipped at one of the water bottles. "How far did you say the museum is from here?" he asked.

"About fifteen kilometers, give or take," Anubis said. "We could probably make it there by foot in three hours. Or…" He frowned and tapped his chin. "The pyramid light show will begin soon, which means buses will be dropping off tourists. If we catch a ride on one, it should take us through downtown Cairo on its way back to the depot."

"Perfect." I would have ridden on a camel through rush hour if it meant getting out of a three-hour walk. After the hellcat ride, I was in serious need of a chiropractor and a hot bath. Saul was going to need some help, too. I doubted even a trip to Hades' Hound House would suffice. I whistled, letting him know snack time was over and we were on the move again.

"Any luck with that scroll?" Anubis asked as we made our way down the hill toward the Sphinx.

"Not really," I admitted. I should have expected that if an Egyptian god couldn't make jackals or scarabs of the charred document, there wasn't much I'd get out of it.

"Ah, well." Anubis shrugged. "Once we have coin in hand, I'll take it back to Duat for Thoth to have a look. He's got a sharp eye for these things."

"What about a sharp weapon?" Bub enquired. "Perhaps it's time to call in reinforcements? I suspect Sekhmet will not be caught off guard a second time."

"I'm sure someone will be willing to accompany us to Taposiris," Anubis said.

"Accompany *you*." Bub gave him a rigid smile. When I shot my demon a dirty look, he added, "We're undecided if we'll be returning."

"I see." Anubis shrugged again. "Then I guess I'll track down that other reaper while I wait for Thoth's assessment of the scroll."

"Let's not get ahead of ourselves." I squeezed his shoulder with my non-mummified hand. "I'm sure we'll catch a second wind after a real meal and a shower."

Bub snorted and picked up the pace, taking the lead as we reached the entrance of the complex. Just as Anubis had predicted, a herd of tourists were unloading from a bus. Many of them wore matching shirts that sported the same Arabic writing as a faded advertisement stretched beneath the bus's windows. I couldn't read it, but I recognized King Tut's famous death mask.

"That's the one we want." Anubis pointed. "Tutankhamun's exhibit is at the museum. That bus should take us right by it. Come on." He waved me along as the last of the tourists exited the vehicle.

I was just glad it wasn't a soda truck. I gripped the strap of my bag and hurried to catch up.

The smelly bus felt like first-class service after spending seven hours crammed between pallets. A cool breeze filtered through the windows, promising nightfall was near. It brushed my crusty curls away from my face. I closed my eyes and stretched my arms over the tops of the surrounding seats, enjoying the ride despite the blare of horns and traffic fumes.

Since we were mostly alone—save for the driver and an older woman singing to herself in the seat behind him—I'd banished Saul to the back row where we wouldn't have to smell his bloody breath and the gore that had dried to his fur.

Bub sat across the aisle, legs kicked up and arms folded. Meanwhile, Anubis dashed back and forth like a rabid border collie, excitedly pointing out a zoo, an opera house, and a high-end hotel that was new since his last visit, sometime in the early nineteen-eighties.

"I just wanted to make sure everything made it back in its rightful place," he explained. "That was after one of the big world tours, and surveillance wasn't quite what it is today."

He rambled on and on about all the riches and relics that had been found in Tut's tomb, including his own shrine, where he kept his emergency stash of coins and a few ancient keepsakes. It was a divine version of an offshore account or safety deposit box. And, evidently, many other deities chose to hide their obsolete talismans and most powerful relics in a similar fashion.

"Would it really be so bad if Sekhmet got her hands on Isis's pearly bits?" Bub pondered aloud. "I thought Hathor was a gentle goddess, fun-loving and motherly."

"Yes, a real heavenly cow," Anubis said, earning a grunt of disapproval from me. "I mean that literally, and affectionately," he clarified. "She was delightful. I haven't the foggiest why she didn't return after the war, but we don't know for certain that Sekhmet's goal is to restore her mother form."

"If that *were* her goal, what would be her next move?" I asked. "Didn't you say something about her needing a cult or coven?"

"Well, yes." Anubis cleared his throat. "But even with a cult, these things take careful planning and time. *Years*, even."

Bub snorted. "If you don't know her intentions, then how would you know how long she's been planning this?"

"Fair point," Anubis said, grabbing the back of a chair as the bus turned around a wide, circular plaza. In the center, an obelisk speared the sky. Anubis squinted at the hieroglyphs spanning the pink granite. "That's new—circa Ramesses the Great, I believe." Then the museum appeared. "There she is," he whispered.

The building's burnt-orange façade was set ablaze with golden spotlights. It was a piece of art in itself, with a dome and arches and statues set high into the façade on either side of the entrance. An oasis of pristine grass and soaring palm trees made up the front lawn. It featured wide sidewalks, a raised pond, and more statues, including a pair of sphinxes, all closed in by a tall, iron fence. The intricate metalwork of the front gate could be seen from a block away, and it was so captivating that it took a moment for me to realize the museum was closed.

"Will the bus stop if there's no one waiting to be picked up?" I asked, reaching for my bag in the seat beside me.

"Not likely." Anubis shot a sheepish grin over his shoulder before sticking his head through one of the open windows. "But the traffic at the next intersection should slow things down enough for us to dismount unscathed."

"Lovely," Bub said, pulling himself up by one of the support poles anchored in the aisle. He opened his hand, inviting me to go ahead of him. I whistled for Saul, and the four of us gathered in close to the exit, preparing for a stealthy departure.

The driver's nose crinkled, and he frowned at the singing woman in the rearview mirror. She scowled right back and fanned a tattered magazine in front of her face. My eyes watered, but I did my best not to gag. *Someone* had definitely farted.

I stared at my hound, marveling in disgust that his odor had been strong enough to seep through the veil and disturb the mortals. His ears lay flat against his head, and he whimpered in protest when I used a single finger to pet his muzzle.

"Here we go," Anubis announced as the bus slowed at the intersection just past the museum.

He'd been right. Horns blared, and tires squealed. Drivers shouted out their windows and threw their hands up. The streets were cramped and hot from so many engines revving in close proximity. I couldn't tell where one lane ended and the next began. There were no lines anywhere.

Anubis touched a finger to his brow in farewell to the driver, even though the man couldn't see him, and hopped off the bus. Bub grabbed my hand and exited a step behind me. Saul waited for me to call him again before leaping into the busy junction. We cut through the slow-moving traffic, making our way to the sidewalk around the museum. From there we circled around to the front of the building and slipped through the fancy gate.

Gold, lion-headed knockers hung from the museum's massive doors. With the sacred treasures housed behind them, I half expected we'd be shut out, unable to thin our soul matter enough to gain entry. But the lion guardians yielded, and we found ourselves in a quiet lobby, the angry traffic outside reduced to a distant hum.

"This way," Anubis said, leading us past the metal detectors. "The Tutankhamun exhibit is on the upper level."

Though the museum had closed some hours ago, soft security lights illuminated the statues and antiquities displayed on raised platforms and in glass cases. The central hall, an atrium from the long row of skylights above, was sunken and bookended by wide stairs. The steps at the far end of the room were divided by a landing that held a gigantic pair of statues, likely of a pharaoh and his queen. Smaller, life-sized pharaohs sat on stone thrones atop elevated platforms around them.

Anubis navigated through the historic maze with increasing speed. We stayed right on his heels, following him to a staircase off the hall behind the atrium.

My heart crept into my throat as we climbed. After the events of the weekend, I couldn't wait to crawl into bed and get a good night's rest. Thoth would need time to analyze the scroll anyway. Since Bub had talked me into requested extra time off, I fully intended to sleep in until Anubis figured out the next stop on this derailed expedition.

There were more display cases on the second floor. Anubis pointed out one that housed an enormous, elaborate gold and blue box.

"The outer shrine of Tutankhamun's mummy. There were four protecting his sarcophagus," he said, opening his hand at the next few cases featuring progressively smaller, golden shrines.

It was strange to think of Winston tucked away in all this finery so very long ago, thousands of years before I knew him. Thousands of years before reapers were tasked with harvesting the dead. I wondered who had collected his soul, or had all his ceremonial treasures pointed him home where Anubis waited to weigh his heart? When had he tired of being revered in paradise and requested reinsertion? I had so many questions, but they would have to wait.

"Finally!" Anubis stopped in front of a case holding a golden shrine. This one was the size of a large trunk. A statue of a black jackal lounged on top, its eyes and ears rimmed with gold. A golden collar and scarf were wrapped around its neck, as well.

Saul grumbled at the life-sized figure. I imagined he was still miffed about Coreen skipping out on guard duty to run off with Anubis's gadabouts. Saul was a stinky beast, but he was obedient, and his tracking skills were second to none.

"Awww," I cooed at Anubis. "You look so dapper with your little scarf."

He tilted his chin in the air and sniffed. "It's a sash, and it symbolizes the loyalty and protection I offer."

"Fancy that." Bub scoffed. "Yet somehow we've nearly died three times on this trip."

"But you didn't," Anubis was quick to point out. "You're alive and well—and here to complain about it."

He circled the case and paused at the ass end of the dog. Long poles extended under the shrine, likely meant for easy transport. The glass case enclosed those as well, leaving enough space for a person to stand inside, directly behind the shrine.

"I'll just be a moment," Anubis said. His soul matter faded, and then he stepped through the glass. Bub and I watched as he twisted the jackal statue's tail to one side, and a hidden compartment popped open. It was a comically clever hiding spot, but apparently not clever enough.

The color drained from Anubis's face, and even the glass couldn't muffle his gasp of horror.

"It's gone!" he shrieked, fisting his hands in his unruly hair. "It's all gone!"

CHAPTER SEVENTEEN

"All strange and terrible events are welcome,
but comforts we despise."
—Shakespeare's Cleopatra

Dᴇsᴘɪᴛᴇ ᴛʜᴇ sʜɪᴛ-ᴛᴀsᴛɪᴄ ᴡᴇᴇᴋᴇɴᴅ we'd had so far—being poisoned, robbed, transported halfway across the country in the back of a hot delivery truck, and then attacked by hellcats—Anubis had remained cool as a corpse. For a death god, he was refreshingly optimistic. I was beginning to think nothing could get under his skin. Who would have thought a missing coin stash would be the straw that broke the jackal's back?

"It's okay," I said, awkwardly adjusting to the role reversal. "We're in Cairo. We passed, like, six hospitals on the way here."

"Precisely." Bub nodded, though a line of worry creased his brow. "We're bound to run into a reaper at any one of them tomorrow, likely by mid-morning."

Anubis stopped his pacing between the display cases and dragged his hands down his face. "I'm afraid that may be time we cannot afford."

"What?" I balked. "You were just talking about taking the scroll back to Duat for Thoth to analyze while we slept off this nightmarish outing."

He thrust a finger at his ransacked shrine. "That was before—"

"I hardly see how your financial woes complicate this harebrained quest," Bub said.

"Financial woes?" Anubis barked out a dry laugh. "This isn't about the missing coin."

"Then what *is* it about?" I demanded.

"A book." He closed his eyes and pinched the bridge of his nose. "The Book of Eternal Breath, which I used to help Isis resurrect Osiris. The spell it holds… is one of the most powerful I've ever crafted. There's a reason I kept the book hidden here in the mortal realm."

"But Hathor's not dead, right?" I blinked at him. "Why would Sekhmet need the book to restore her mother form?"

"She wouldn't."

"Maybe Sekhmet's not responsible for this particular crime then," Bub suggested. "You said you haven't been here for some decades."

"Well, whoever *did* do this has something much worse planned than reviving an extinct goddess," Anubis said. "My leopard skin cloak is missing, too."

Bub frowned. "Meaning…?"

"The skin once belonged to Seth. He transformed himself into a leopard and tried to attack Osiris. I flayed him and paraded about in his skin as warning to his followers and those who would rob the dead."

"Brutal." I shook my head, trying to dislodge the gory image. "And why would Sekhmet—or anyone— need *that?*"

"I can think of only one reason." Anubis's brows drew together. His gaze was suddenly hollow, distant. "To resurrect Seth."

"No." The word escaped me like a yelp after a bee sting. It was more gut reaction than a conscious denial. I couldn't believe Anubis. I *refused* to believe him. "It's impossible. Seth was mutilated, dismembered."

"So was Osiris, but Isis and I brought him back." Anubis shrugged. "If Sekhmet already has the book and the cloak, and then she gets her hands on Isis's talisman…" His gaze went out of focus again, and he swallowed hard.

"But he'd come back as a mortal, right?" I said. "So eventually, he'd die, and then a reaper would be sent to collect the soul he's attached to." I thought of the time I'd mistakenly been sent to harvest Odin. Of course,

Odin had been born in a mortal vessel. No ritual sacrifices or cults required. I supposed that made it an apples to oranges comparison, but I was desperate.

"That's not how the spell or the talisman work." Anubis sighed. "Both bypass the need for psychopompic intervention. Yes, Seth would eventually die as mortals do. At which point, the spirit of his possessed vessel would be destroyed to forge a bridge to Eternity, and Seth would emerge in his divine form in Duat, his native realm."

"And you think someone is planning to pull off this resurrection tonight?" Bub's frown deepened. "How can you be so sure?"

"I'd love to be wrong, trust me." Anubis rubbed a hand over his face. His overgrown stubble and the dark circles under his eyes made him look more unhinged than divine. "But with Sekhmet's solar powers as the Eye of Ra, it will undoubtedly be a sunrise ritual."

Nausea gripped my insides, and I folded my arms over my stomach. "How are we supposed to get to Taposiris. I don't think we'll be lucky enough to find another delivery truck driver, at least not this late in the evening."

"You can't be serious." Bub grabbed my shoulder and pulled me back a step, away from Anubis and the case with the looted shrine. "We barely survived that last encounter with Sekhmet. You're injured, and we're almost out of supplies. And now, she'll be expecting us—and she'll be counting on us bringing backup."

"Exactly," Anubis said, eyes widening with some epiphany. "She probably thinks we'll take the time to assemble an army. This is our only chance to catch her off guard and stop this madness."

"*This* is the madness I'd like to stop," Bub said, his voice hitching an octave. "Have you both lost your minds? We have no coin, no weapons—"

"We did just fine without either at the pyramids," Anubis said, earning an infuriated glare from my demon.

"Just fine? I'm sorry, are we talking about the same battle? The one where we were almost eaten by hellcats?"

At the mention of hellcats, Saul's ears perked. He glanced around the museum and let out a soft *woof*. I scratched his head, forgetting the tacky blood dried in his fur.

"If Sekhmet's not expecting us for another day or two, then maybe we can be sneaky about this and avoid another battle," I suggested.

"Do you think so?" Bub turned his scorching sarcasm on me. "Say we do collect all these dusty trinkets, and let's say we even make it out alive and hitch a ride to a hospital. Where do you suppose Sekhmet and whatever henchmen she brings will look for us first? Hell, they may even be waiting for us, since *they* have coin to get around."

"Fair points," I said, attempting to quell his mounting hysteria. "But maybe the coin stash is with the book and cloak?" I turned to Anubis, hoping for some reassurance, or at least a break from Bub's scathing gaze. The god's brow furrowed. He opened his mouth, hesitating until he caught my pointed stare.

"Sure, it's possible," he said, lacking the ironclad conviction that probably wouldn't have convinced Bub anyway.

"So how are we getting to Taposiris?" I asked again as if the matter were settled.

"The train station isn't far from here." Anubis headed back toward the stairs and waved for us to follow. "It's a three-hour ride to Alexandria. Then we'll have to find another vehicle to take us the rest of the way."

"Great." Bub threw his hands in the air. "There are half a dozen hospitals within walking distance, but you'd rather take your chances with mortal transportation than wait for a reaper."

"A train has to be more comfortable than sitting on pallets in the back of a delivery truck," I offered. "I bet it's more comfortable than plastic hospital chairs, too." I turned my focus to the stairs and grabbed the railing, avoiding his cynical scowl. The truth was a little messier than I wanted to admit.

Turning Isis down in the first place was one thing. And yes, maybe I'd let my resentment toward Tasha and my desire to please the Woke Souls overrule my better judgment. But now I was too invested. I had to see this through. Otherwise, I'd risked everything for nothing.

If we went back to Duat empty-handed and begged for reinforcements, how could I claim this victory as my own? Sure, I wasn't exactly alone now. But Anubis served as a guide, and Bub was my hopeful consort. Saul was my trusty hound. Anyone else would expect credit due where credit was owed.

Was it a selfish and reckless outlook? Absolutely. Was I still counting on earning deity brownie points with Isis? You betcha. Would I survive long enough to cash in those points for a goddess upgrade? Well… I always had relied more on luck than brains. Hopefully that strategy would keep me afloat a little longer.

The real question was, what were we going to do with Seth if we didn't make it to Taposiris in time to stop Sekhmet from resurrecting him? I had no doubt he'd off himself the second he rose in the flesh. I didn't want to think about the mayhem that would ensue once he dropped in unannounced on Isis and company in their newly renovated realm.

The demented old god had been a pain in my ass when he'd been alive, but Grim Thanatos had struck him down, and in gruesome fashion. That I'd been the one to end Grim should have instilled confidence, but I was blinded by doubt. I couldn't see past stopping Sekhmet. If I failed to do that...

Well. I guess *then* I'd suffer through an *I told you so* from Bub. If Seth didn't put me out of my misery first.

At least my pride and ambition didn't deserve all the blame for rushing to storm the castle—er, tomb. If Anubis was right, and there wasn't a moment to lose, we had to stop Seth from coming back. He'd been the catalyst for the Second War of Eternity. The cornerstone of so much death and destruction from which Limbo City was still recovering. I wasn't ready to let fear forfeit our hard-won peace. Not yet.

We reached the ground level of the museum, and Anubis directed us back toward the atrium, navigating the stairs and aisles between the statues, stone sarcophagi, and glass cases. He made it halfway through the room and stopped so suddenly, I nearly ran him over.

Two dark figures stood at the top of the steps leading up to the lobby. Saul's muzzle tapped my thigh, and he growled softly.

"Are those *statues*?" I whispered, trying to recall if they'd been there when we'd arrived.

"Yes," Anubis said under his breath, his tone terse and uncertain.

"What's the problem?" Bub asked, poking his head over my shoulder to have a better look. The museum lights had dimmed, and shadows puddled under every-thing.

"There's another exit," Anubis began, turning back the way we'd come. His mouth dropped open, and I spun around.

Three more statues waited at the foot of the steps we'd just descended. One was missing most of her face, another an arm. They stood perfectly still while my nerves tried to crawl out of my skin.

"Uh… were those there before?" I asked.

"Isn't the lion Sekhmet's token mascot?" Bub added, squinting at one of the figures' crumbled features.

The ones that hadn't been fully defaced did resemble lions. Not quite the goddess I'd become acquainted with, but the animal-headed deities had relinquished those attributes to headdresses long ago.

"That's her, all right," Anubis answered. "This could be a problem."

"I thought your powers were diminished on the mortal side," I said, my gaze darting from one end of the hall to the other.

"Yes, but there are exceptions." Anubis's jaw flexed. "Power can be stolen or borrowed. It can be siphoned from artifacts, or summoned from within them to manipulate. There are laws against it, but I think we've already established what little regard Sekhmet has for rules. She must have known we'd come here and discover her deceit, so she set a snare to keep us from thwarting her plans."

"They're not moving," Bub said, his head twisting back and forth.

I gritted my teeth. "I think I'd feel better if they did." The statues' stalemate stares were creeping me out.

Saul's shoulder pressed in against the back of my knee, and his growl dissolved into a confused whine. I scratched between his ears again as I scanned the room. A short wall surrounded the sunken hall, topped with pillars that held up the floor above. I searched the nearby platforms and statues, assessing which ones could be climbed for a quick exit through gaps between the columns. From there, I was sure I could find a side door out of the museum.

Anubis followed my gaze and sucked in a sharp breath. "It could work, but I would be remiss if I didn't offer fair warning. Amenhotep the Third was a big fan of Sekhmet's."

"Well, he was clearly stupid," I snapped.

"Perhaps," Anubis said. "I only tell you this because he commissioned at least six hundred statues of the goddess in his time. I'm not entirely sure how many of them are housed in this gallery."

"Swell." I eyed the columns again and readjusted my bag across my back, tightening the straps. "We should split up. Maybe it will confuse them."

"I don't know that your holy fire will do much against stone," Bub said.

"I was planning on running," I admitted. My grim, soul-zapping ability had been a gamble with the hellcat. I wasn't ready to test my luck again so soon. Even if the statues were fueled by some sort of soul matter that I could unravel, there was a good chance I'd be crushed to death before finding out.

"Should we count to three?" Bub asked. His hand found mine and squeezed, betraying his lack of faith in this slapdash plan. Even in the thin light, I could see the sweat rising on his brow.

Anubis dipped his chin in a stiff nod as if he were afraid too much motion would trigger an attack. "If they give chase beyond the museum, follow El-Galaa Street to the northeast. It will take you right past the train station. We can meet up there."

"Got it." I glanced down at Saul, trying to recall if we'd covered a Latin command for *run like hell*. I hoped he'd get the gist once we all made for the exits.

"One?" Bub began, glancing between Anubis and me before continuing. "Two. Three!"

My heart shot up into my throat as I bolted for a nearby sarcophagus and climbed atop it. Saul yipped at my heels, having followed me rather than the others. I didn't have time to consider if he'd be able to scale the monuments before something clamped around my ankle, and I was yanked off my feet.

I sucked in a surprised breath that immediately rushed back out as I belly-flopped onto the sarcophagus. The grip on my ankle tightened, and then I was suddenly airborne. What little air I had left to spare wheezed past my lips as my backside smashed through a wide display case in the center of the room.

Glass shards rained all around me, covering the slab of ancient stone it had once sheltered. My bag mostly protected my shoulder blades, but my skull throbbed, and the metallic taste of blood stung the back of my throat. I'd bitten my tongue. But at least my ankle was free.

I squinted up at the jagged hole my body had made in the display case and caught a glimpse of the Sekhmet statue responsible. She was already turning away, looking for another target. Her stone feet hovered soundlessly over the museum floor. Saul barked and pranced a nervous circle around her, but she paid him no attention.

"Cursed fiends!" Anubis shouted, presumably at whichever statues had confronted him. Though I hadn't heard anything else smash, so he was managing better than I.

I groaned and sat up, instantly regretting it when my vision blurred. Then Bub appeared, reaching a hand through the broken glass to help me stand. As soon as I was upright, he inspected my bandaged wrist, turning it over to make sure the dressing hadn't come undone.

"I guess demons and hellhounds don't count," he said, sounding more relieved than offended. He picked a shard of glass away from my hair and dusted another off my blouse before wrapping his hands around my middle and lifting me out of the case.

"Why do I count?" I complained, gingerly touching the back of my head.

Bub smirked at the question. "Spells have no use for titles on paper, pet. Power recognizes power. You're a goddess in all the ways that count."

"A little help here?" Anubis called.

We found him on the opposite side of the room. Three of the Sekhmets surrounded an elevated statue of a pharaoh seated on a throne. Anubis sat in the man's lap, legs pulled up out of reach and arms wrapped around the statue's neck.

The other two Sekhmet statues still guarded the stairs leading up to the lobby, though their bodies had rotated in my direction.

"If ever there was a need, love…" Bub tsked and tapped his toe on the side of my boot, reminding me of the skeleton coin.

It seemed so obvious, but I'd resisted using it for ten years. Now, it rarely even crossed my mind as an option. I supposed it was finally time. I rested my foot on the busted frame of the display case and twisted the heel, revealing the hidden compartment.

There was nothing unique about the coin's appearance. I kept it in a special place mostly so I wouldn't accidentally spend it on a cup of coffee. And also in case I was mugged and left stranded, like Sekhmet had done to us in Dendera. But even then, I had refrained.

I couldn't decide if the decision was driven more by pride or fear. Pride that I'd made do all this time without relying on it. Or fear that it might not work, that the last of its magic had died along with the throne that had forged it.

Heads or tails, I thought grimly. Then, before I could lose my nerve, I flipped the coin in the air.

CHAPTER EIGHTEEN

*"It is normal for me to wake and find myself writing in the
dark... or to be out of my tomb, caught in an unearthly world,
alive with the images that haunt me."*
—Kim Elizabeth

DISAPPOINTMENT WAS AN ODDLY vague word for the
spectrum of emotions it covered. There was the mildly
annoying disappointment of a vending machine being
out of your favorite candy bar. Then the sweat-inducing
disappointment of missing an elevator when you're running late for a meeting. Or the gut-wrenching
disappointment of being betrayed.

In that regard, disappointment was a disappointing
word. And it didn't even begin to express the way I felt
when absolutely *nothing* happened after I flipped Winston's coin.

"Maybe you did it wrong," Bub said under his breath
as the two Sekhmet statues guarding the lobby descended the stairs. "Try again."

I turned the coin over in my hand and gave it another
flip. Still nothing. Then I rolled it across my knuckles in

traditional reaper fashion before attempting the flashier parlor tricks used to impress departing souls. Each failure sank my heart deeper and deeper, and seemed to hasten the Sekhmet statues who had turned their attention on me.

"Is that a coin?" Anubis shouted from his perch. "You've had a coin this *whole* time?"

"It doesn't work," I hissed.

"Out of marks, but worth a shot," Bub lied on my behalf since I was still fuming. "We need a new plan, but for now—" He glanced up at a raised statue of a pharaoh on a throne. It was similar to the one Anubis had sought refuge on.

I didn't fancy the idea of cowering, but I was already feeling slightly concussed from my first encounter with the stone wardens.

Bub cupped his hands, and I stepped into them, bracing myself on his shoulders until he hefted me into the air. I landed squarely in the pharaoh's lap and winced at the sharp pain in my tailbone. The bruise must have come from my collision with the glass case. I was sure I'd be feeling the aftermath of that ride well into next week.

Bub inched away from the monument as the Sekhmet statues closed in. He clicked his tongue, encouraging Saul to back away, as well. But other than cornering me, the statues didn't seem interested in inflicting more violence. Same for the ones surrounding Anubis.

"If you don't attempt to leave, it appears you're safe from harm," Bub said. "I could head to the nearest hospital and bum a coin off the first reaper who appears."

Anubis made a frustrated noise in the back of his throat. "And the power imbuing them will run out sooner or later too, but both options take too much time. The fact that Sekhmet left this trap for us only confirms how soon she intends to raise Seth."

"Do you still have that rope?" I asked Bub.

His brows dropped into a humorless line. "Haven't you played Pecos Bill enough for one day?"

"It's not for me." I pointed up at the balustrade wrapped around the second-floor opening above the hall we were trapped in. "You're going to pull Anubis over that railing so he can resurrect his shrine Fido and distract these stone-cold bitches until we make our escape."

"I'm going to what now?" Bub folded his arms.

"That could work," Anubis agreed. "Though I'd have to break the same rule Sekhmet did to activate her idols."

"I won't tell if you don't," I said.

"You know, I believe I have another idol on this level with second-floor overlook access," Anubis added. "We could drop in there after stopping by the shrine."

"Even better."

"He's not quite to scale as Sekhmet's minions."

"We're not placing bets on who's going to win," I snapped. "We only need a little smoke and mirror action."

"I know. I just hate to throw him to the lions." Anubis sighed. "Seems it's the season for sacrifices."

"And I'm about to sacrifice my lower back pulling your arse up to bloody heaven," Bub grumbled as he dug the rope out of his bag. He spared us each a dirty look before heading off toward the back stairs. "Don't thank me all at once for being the only one with the foresight to bring basic survival gear."

"Thank you!" Anubis and I shouted at the same time. I resisted the urge to tack on *Your Profane Darkness* like the Styx Stop waitress had. His mood was sour enough.

In the awkward silence that followed, Anubis and I passed the time trading uncomfortable glances with our keepers and each other in our undignified roles as pharaonic lapdogs. When Bub finally appeared at the second-floor railing, his expression changed to one of amusement.

"You're like a couple of telltales being bullied at the playground, run off to your mummies. *Mummies.*" He cackled before taking a closer look. "Maybe I should pull Lana up first, since she weighs less. Then we could heave-ho the *top dog* together," he said, cocking his head toward Anubis.

"I should stay here to keep an eye on our new friends." I nodded at the statues. "If one of them makes a move to head your way, I'll shout a warning."

"And I'm not *that* much heavier." Anubis tilted his chin in the air.

"Fine." Bub rolled his eyes and tossed one end of the rope over the railing. Anubis knotted it around his waist before standing on his pharaoh savior's lap. He dipped his head at the statue and winced.

"Apologies for the disrespect," he said. "Please forgive me for this unintended slight."

"I'm sure he'll get over it." Bub yanked on his end of the rope impatiently. "And the sooner we get *you* over this railing, the sooner we can get the hell out of here."

Anubis huffed, but he stepped onto the statue's shoulders, then its crowned head. It gave him more height than I'd expected, though Bub still grunted with effort once the god's full weight was upon him. My demon pressed a boot to the railing and leaned backward, straining as his hands turned red around the rope. Anubis held on tight and planted his sandaled feet on the nearest pillar as the Sekhmet statues that had been babysitting him gathered below. Their unblinking stares followed his progression, but they didn't attempt to reach for his legs.

Escape from the second floor was unlikely, and their purpose was apparently only to keep us here. They hadn't been instructed to seek and destroy. Maybe Sekhmet respected the museum too much to sully them with our blood and guts, the same way she respected Hathor's temple in Dendera. Though one of the stone hags who was still staring me down had swung me like a bat into a display case. Unpleasant as that had been, she'd left me alone after preventing me from escaping into the adjacent hall.

"Ha-ha!" Anubis cheered as he flopped over the second-floor railing. Bub groaned out a sound that was less victory and more relief. "Let's get to work!" Anubis said, clapping him on the shoulder.

"*You* get to work," Bub snarled. "I just did my part."

Their voices faded as they headed off toward the god's shrine.

When I looked back down, all five statues surrounded the base of my elevated sanctuary, their wide eyes staring up at me. I tightened my arms around the pharaoh's neck and pulled my legs up farther out of reach. My bruised tailbone complained again. I gritted my teeth, praying Anubis knew what he was doing.

In the meantime, I was a damsel in distress, waiting to be rescued and bored to death. Every passing second felt longer than the last. If I ended up stuck here until morning, I was going to lose my mind. I frowned at my stone companion and jerked my chin at the crowd assembled beneath his throne.

"Friends of yours?" I asked, wondering how closely he was related to the pharaoh who'd had his head stuck up Sekhmet's ass. If he'd been inclined to answer me, his response would have been interrupted by an unearthly howl that echoed throughout the museum, ear-splitting as a fire alarm.

"*That* would be a friend of *mine*." I smirked at the statues, though they were too unaffected to care about my gloating. Their blank gazes angled toward the back stairs that led down into the hall as the gold-trimmed jackal from Anubis's shrine appeared.

Saul barked in surprise, recognizing the previously inanimate idol. The little beast let loose with another howl, cutting it short when one of the Sekhmets launched herself at him. He leapt over her, on top of a stone sarcophagus, and then through an opening between two columns, escaping into the next hall.

A second Sekhmet joined the first that had broken from the pride. The two of them split off in opposite directions, following the wall that stood between them and their new quarry. That still left three statues for me to contend with, which was three too many in my professional opinion.

Something crashed in the neighboring hall, and then the gilded jackal soared through another pair of columns, back into the atrium. His lean body easily navigated the monuments, then vanished over the wall on the opposite side of the room, into another hall just beyond.

A third Sekhmet left to join the hunt. Shortly after, the first two statues that had chased the jackal darted through the lobby in hot pursuit. As limber as Anubis's canine idol was, I knew he wouldn't last long. Which meant, if I was going to make a run for it, my window of opportunity was waning, too.

I groaned and glanced down at the remaining two Sekhmets, wondering what my odds were of making it through the museum's front doors before they used me to finish smashing what was left of the glass case in the center of the room.

Before I could do anything too stupid, the sound of stone scratching on stone echoed through the museum. I scanned the room, searching for the source of the racket.

At the back of the hall, where the largest statues of a pharaoh and his queen dominated a landing in the center of the stairs, a dark figure clumsily scaled the side of their throne. I could have sworn I heard him grunt with the effort he was making. When he reached the pharaoh's lap and turned toward us, a spotlight splashed over his face, revealing a jackal snout. He stamped a foot on the pharaoh's outspread hand, chipping away at his stone fingers.

One of the Sekhmets darted away from my perch to go after him. To my surprise and horror, she began to climb the base of the monument. The pint-sized Anubis climbed higher, up onto the pharaoh's shoulder, all the while punching and kicking at the statues delicately chiseled features.

With only one Sekhmet left, I doubted I'd have a better chance to make my escape. I braced myself against my own pharaoh's shoulders and rose into a squatting position as I searched for the best place to land—or *fall*, rather. From this height, there would be nothing graceful about the way I hit the floor.

"Wait!"

My gaze shot up to the second floor in time to watch Bub toss a loop of rope down over me and my pharaoh perch. It enclosed the remaining Sekhmet, too. Right before Bub yanked it tight, pinning her to the base of the monument with a grating crunch. He quickly wrapped the rope around the railing, gripped the loose end in both hands, and dropped into the hall, using his own body as a counterweight to trap the statue.

"Now!" Bub shouted.

I didn't need to be told twice. My knees wobbled as my boots hit the lid of the nearest sarcophagus, but I managed to slide to the floor without losing my balance. The sound of grinding stone and creaking rope spurred me forward. I raced for the front stairs, refusing to look back.

Every second was precious now. Each breath stabbed at my heart, already working double-time against my panic as I dodged around monuments. I rushed up the stairs and forged ahead despite the encroaching darkness of tunnel vision.

A faint exit light illuminated the front doors in red. I was so close.

"Gah!" Anubis shrieked as he slammed into my side. Another jolt of adrenaline ripped through me as I hit the floor.

"Jesus," I wheezed, pressing a hand to my chest. He grabbed my free arm and yanked me to my feet, just as a pair of Sekhmet statues in the hall he'd emerged from turned toward us.

"Go! Go! Go!" Anubis shoved me toward the doors.

I was so frazzled, my soul matter almost didn't thin in time. At the last second, I slipped through and collapsed onto the concrete steps outside. Anubis flopped down beside me, panting and cackling hysterically.

"We made it," he said, grinning with relief.

"Did we?" I asked. We both yelped as Bub and Saul emerged from the building.

"Please, hold your applause," Bub said, offering up a grandiose bow.

I glanced past him at the museum doors. "They can't get to us out here, right?"

"No, no." Anubis shook his head. "Well, I don't think so."

"You don't *think* so?" I scoffed.

As if prompted, something heavy slammed against the door, rattling the lion-headed knockers. Saul barked a warning as Anubis and I scrambled to our feet.

"Maybe we don't stick around to find out?" Bub offered.

"Right," Anubis said. "Besides, we've got a train to catch."

CHAPTER NINETEEN

"And how can man die better than facing fearful odds,
for the ashes of his fathers, and the temples of his Gods?"
—Thomas Babington Macaulay

THE LATE-NIGHT TRAIN FROM CAIRO to Alexandria was a welcome luxury and reprieve from the non-stop chaos we'd encountered since Dendera. My aching body melted into the cushioned seat, and the hum of wheels on endless tracks threatened to lull me to sleep. A three-hour nap sounded like a swell idea. My batteries were in definite need of recharging.

Bub sat beside me, seat reclined and hat covering his face, a clear indicator that he'd settled in for a rest, too. There were maybe half a dozen mortals scattered throughout the car. The darkness beyond the train windows left little for them to do besides stare into their phones or doze. Either way, it seemed we were in for a quiet ride.

"I bet she was meeting someone in Giza," Anubis blurted, jarring me from my sleepy daze. The exhilaration of our recent survival and escape had worn off, and he'd returned to the task of unraveling Sekhmet's deceit. "That's the only thing that makes sense," he went on, talking more to himself than anyone else. "All she needed was at the museum. There was no reason for her to be at the pyramids unless she wanted somewhere flashy to meet an accomplice."

Bub lifted his hat off his face and glared at Anubis. "Which only confirms that we shouldn't be going into this bullheaded and without backup."

"Perhaps another deity with feline influence," the god said, ignoring my demon's commentary. "That might explain the hellcats and the power she would have needed to command five full-sized idols. Summoning two *small* statues was a tall order for me."

"Then what makes you think we stand a chance against her at Taposiris?" Bub demanded. "You do hear the words coming out of your own mouth, do you not?"

"Like I can go back to Duat now with nothing to show for it." Anubis snorted. "Unless you count the heap of desecrated relics at the museum. The only way I—that *we*—don't end up as disgraced laughingstocks in this situation is if we finish what we started and retrieve Isis's talisman."

"Which could also end up being the only way we stop Sekhmet from resurrecting Seth," I said, cuing a dramatic gape of betrayal from Bub. "What? It's true." I blinked at him, refusing to cower to anything so useless as basic survival instincts.

Saul, who had stretched out on his belly down the aisle, groaned and threw one of his enormous paws over his muzzle. It took a lot to earn his ire, but running low on treats and sleep was the fastest way to get there. He slowly rose to his feet and trotted off to the rear of the train car before flopping back down with an annoyed grunt.

"We should find a hospital in Alexandria, wait for a reaper, and request assistance from the Nephilim Guard," Bub said.

"We've been through too much to give up now." I sighed and leaned my head back on the seat cushion. So much for that catnap.

"You're free to do as you wish," Anubis said. "But I'll be going after Sekhmet. It's not just about my reputation. She intends to use my cloak and my spell to commit treason. If she succeeds in bringing Seth back, I'll never forgive myself. Isis may not either."

Bub twisted in his seat to face me and dropped his voice, cutting Anubis out of the conversation. "You know I want to be your consort, pet, but this is getting out of hand. I am no coward, but I am also not an idiot. I don't fancy rushing into danger when I'm ill-equipped to protect you."

"There are other ways to help besides protecting me," I said, my jaw clenching involuntarily. I looked away, choosing to stare out the darkened window instead.

The damsel treatment always rubbed me wrong. Bub didn't resort to it often, but I tried to let it slide since I could tell he was anxious about his stunted powers. I wouldn't have been thrilled about going up against Sekhmet with one hand tied behind my back either. Not that it would have stopped me.

If Seth hadn't entered the equation, maybe I'd have been more willing to abandon Anubis and let Tasha claim a second victory at my expense. Maybe the tabloids would've overlooked my involvement, and Cordelia and the Woke Souls would have been content by the effort I'd made, however futile. Hell, maybe another opportunity would have arisen for me to forge an alliance with a different goddess—possibly even one without flaming hoops for me to jump through.

But that was an awful lot of maybes. And none of them would matter if I had to live with the fact that I'd let Seth return without doing everything in my power to prevent it.

"Look, I won't hold it against you if you want to go to a hospital and wait it out, but I just can't," I said, my voice softening with regret. "We'll find another way to validate you as my consort… If that's something you still want?" I added timidly when he didn't reply. "Bub?" I turned to find him staring up at the ceiling with milky eyes.

"Shhh," he whispered, pressing a finger to his lips. Sweat glistened on his brow, and for a moment I worried he was under attack from someone or something I couldn't see.

"Bub," I hissed again. His free hand found mine and squeezed. Before my panic went full-blown, a tiny fly buzzed through the train car and landed on the tip of his pointed finger. It paced the edge of his nail as it relayed some buggy message only my demon could understand.

"Very good," Bub said once the fly had finished. It buzzed a short farewell and then disappeared in a tiny puff of yellow smoke.

"I thought your powers didn't work on the mortal side," I said.

"They are limited." He nodded stiffly, recovering from the effort the feat had taken. "But there is an Abrahamic loophole that suggests all pagan faiths are rooted in Hell, fostered by demons in disguise." He grinned at my delighted relief and then winked. "I know how to bend a rule or two myself, love. There are other ways to help, right?"

"So it would appear." I leaned across the arm rest between our seats and kissed his cheek since he was still regaining his breath.

I'd meant what I'd said about letting him off the hook, but I should have known he'd never take the easy way out. Not where we were concerned. I'd risked everything to save him from Seth's rebel forces, and he'd been prepared to go AWOL with me when the Afterlife Council had nearly voted off with my head. Official or not, we were consorts through and through.

"Well?" Anubis said, reminding us he was still there, waiting across the aisle for an update. "Did you learn anything useful?"

"As a matter of fact, I did." Bub sniffed at the god's impatience. "There is a small group of amateur archaeologists aboard the train car ahead of us who are staying at a resort near Taposiris Magna. They've commissioned a private bus to take them from the station. We should be able to hitch a ride with their lot."

"That *is* useful. Well done!" Anubis cheered and slapped him on the shoulder.

Bub shrugged him off with a grimace. "I'm not doing this for you or your mother's misplaced pearls. And just to be clear, we're grabbing the goods and getting the hell out of there. No heroics." He pointed at Anubis and then me. "Both of you. Understand? We weren't tasked with capturing or assassinating fiends. We're there merely to thwart their dastardly plans."

"Got it." I crossed a finger over my heart and sealed the promise with another kiss, this one on his down-turned mouth. Bub tried very hard to maintain his stern expression, even when I flicked my tongue over his bottom lip.

"You're as stubborn as they come," he said, sighing as the sharp lines of his face softened. "You know that, don't you?"

"I thought you *fancied* my *tenacity*," I teased, imitating his British accent.

"Only in the bedroom, pet." Bub hitched a brow at me and reclined back in his seat. "And I mean it about dodging this fight."

I supposed Sekhmet's ass-kicking could wait. As long as we kept her from resurrecting Seth, I could restrain my wrath a while longer. Couldn't I?

The concession cued a dark little voice in the back of my mind, a voice that reminded me my soul matter-demolishing ability worked just fine. And though I hadn't consumed the hellcat's essence in Giza, I *had* absorbed Grim's soul matter and the power of the throne. Sure, it had been too much for me to hold on to for very long. But that had been an isolated incident that in no way defined the scope of my talent.

What would consuming a force as potent as Sekhmet be like? Would her soul matter be easier to contain and control? I couldn't help but wonder.

Villainous as the goddess had become, I supposed there was still an ethical element to consider. Even self-defense was a slippery slope when it came to my unsanctioned abilities.

"Let's have another look at that scroll," Anubis said, unhitching the drop-down table fixed to the seat in front of him.

"You have another look," I replied, tossing my bag over the aisle. "I'm so tired, my eyes are crossing." I made a face at him to prove it.

Bub had already repositioned his fedora over his face. A muffled snore filtered through the gaps in the straw. The sound compelled a yawn from me that was interrupted when Anubis tossed my bag back into my lap.

"Rude," I muttered under my breath.

"Sorry." He snorted, punctuating how *not* sorry he was, and unfurled the charred scroll. "I'll wake you when we get there, Sleeping Beauty."

"I'm aiming for goddess, not princess," I reminded him. "And for the record, I would have eaten Maleficent alive."

Anubis snorted again, but he turned his gaze down at the blackened papyrus. "I don't doubt that, Lady Death."

The cozy ride did make for a decent nap. Unfortunately, it also gave my body just enough time to acknowledge all the abuse I'd put it through over the past few days. I felt every bruise like a throbbing beacon of defeat as we stepped off the train and shuffled after the co-eds who'd come to see the latest ancient wonders that had been unearthed.

We squeezed into their chartered bus, and I ended up sitting on Bub's lap for the hour-long ride. Not nearly as comfortable as the train or even the city bus in Cairo, but I didn't complain. I was too busy holding my breath. We were all in desperate need of showers. Saul was the only one who didn't seem affected by our overly ripe condition, but he was a connoisseur of stenches.

"They found coins with her face on them," one of our mortal accomplices shouted, escalating a discussion at the front of the bus of which I'd only caught bits and pieces.

"Everyone had coins with her face on them," another young man replied. "That proves nothing."

"They had gold tongues!"

"Knock it off," a woman berated them. "It doesn't matter. This is still a fascinating discovery, regardless of *whom* they found."

Another discussion between two different co-eds began, this time in Arabic, and I was unable to follow along. I closed my eyes and drifted in and out, catching a bit more rest before we finally arrived at the resort near the dig site.

Thankfully, Anubis didn't suggest we wait for the bus to slow down and jump. None of us were in any condition for that. When the vehicle's engine died, we waited for the mortals to spill out into the parking lot, and then took our leave.

I'd lost my flashlight in Dendera, but Bub still had his. He clicked it on as soon as we'd crossed the highway and began up a steep hill. It was dark, but I could see the faint outline of a large structure in the distance.

Nighttime was cooler this close to the Mediterranean Sea. I shivered and tightened my grip on the straps of my bag, hugging it closer to my back. Saul snuggled in against my legs as we climbed, lending me his warmth and stability on the rocky terrain.

"Taposiris Magna," Anubis announced, opening his hand at the looming temple complex as we neared. "The great tomb of Osiris. The north entrance is inaccessible. We'll have to circle around to the east side."

Though the towering block wall had endured, it was in rough shape and nowhere near as decorative as Dendera. It was more the size and position atop the hill that gave it an air of significance. This was not one of the typical tourist attractions with strict security measures and swarms of vendors selling novelty trinkets. There were no god-faced pillars or broken statues on display, no camels waiting to give rides. If it weren't for the recent discoveries, Taposiris could have easily sat for another thousand years without anyone giving it a second glance.

But somewhere within these ruins, in a crypt deep beneath the desert floor, Isis's last mortal vessel and the pieces of her talisman waited for us. We'd made it. Not that we knew exactly where to go, but at least we were here. What had once been the most worrisome aspect of this venture was nothing considering all we'd survived.

Anubis directed us east up the rocky slope and around the corner of the temple complex. The ground was still questionable, but it was easier to manage with one hand on the wall for guidance. A twisted ankle would not make for easy climbing or navigating through subterranean tunnels.

Before we made it much further, Anubis stopped suddenly and swatted at the beam of Bub's flashlight.

"Turn that off," he hissed. "Someone's here."

In the darkness, I could just barely make out the opening in the block wall, softly illuminated by the glow of the resort behind us. But I couldn't hear whatever Anubis had over the pounding of my pulse in my ears.

I inched forward, relying on Saul to keep me from falling in a hole or stepping on a snake. I could sense Bub and Anubis creeping in closer, too. At this range, it was impossible to tell if we were dealing with snooping mortals or a vengeful goddess.

I *really* hoped it was just nosy humans. Otherwise, I had a feeling I'd be too tempted to break my promise to Bub. He was a forgiving demon, but any missteps on my part would be better dealt with *after* we'd collected the talisman. A little victory vengeance would be far more excusable then.

Despite my resistance, as we flanked the break in the temple wall, and Sekhmet's sharp voice cut through the night air, hot wrath tickled my palm.

The goddess had drugged and robbed us before leaving us stranded in Dendera. Then she'd attacked us with hellcats in Giza and possessed idols at the museum in Cairo. The urge to remove her head from her body was strong, and it only intensified as we drew closer.

CHAPTER TWENTY

"Life is not easy for any of us. But what of that?
We must have perseverance and above all confidence in ourselves.
We must believe that we are gifted for something
and that this thing must be attained."
—Marie Curie

It took every ounce of patience I possessed not to poke my head around the corner to see what we were up against. I was dying to know who could stand Sekhmet enough to partner with her in the mythical sedition of the century. Of course, no light seeped past the entrance, so a looksee wouldn't have done much good anyway.

Whoever waited on the other side of the crumbling wall was carrying on their discussion by starlight alone. Luckily, the subject was getting heated—and therefore loud enough to eavesdrop. I tried to pretend this was proper reconnaissance and not cowardice.

"Where is the cult you promised?" a husky, feminine voice demanded.

"Their priest is setting up in the tomb now," Sekhmet said. "The others will be here before sunrise."

"They better be," the mystery woman replied. "I've carried you through this endeavor long enough."

"How dare you!" Sekhmet hissed. "I'm the one who secured the scroll containing the talisman's location."

"The scroll you lost in Giza?" The woman snorted. "You're lucky I was there to assist you. And you owe me two cats. They are harder to rally now that the borders have been fortified."

Son of a bitch.

Anubis was right. Sekhmet *had* stopped in Giza to meet someone. I supposed that made Bub right, too. The Sumerians weren't done causing trouble yet. And whoever this broad was, she could still call on hellcats despite the fact I'd killed the scorpion-tailed lion mount she'd been shepherding the herd with.

My palm flooded with more heat at the revelation, until Bub's hand closed over my wrist. Cold dread curdled my insides at the thought of what my touch could do to him. I sucked in a silent gasp and jerked my arm away, only then realizing that my closed fist had begun to glow. The hellish light reflected in my demon's wide eyes and faded like cooling embers as I smothered my rage.

I swallowed and glanced over my shoulder at Anubis. If he'd noticed, he wasn't saying anything. None of us were while Sekhmet and her fellow killer cat lady were bickering inside the temple walls.

"Careful, *sukkal*," Sekhmet said, her voice tapering into a growl. "This resurrection does not happen without my divine influence. I'd hate to think how your mistress might react if you hinder the rebirth of her long-lost consort."

"And where will you seek refuge if you fail, pussycat?" the woman taunted. "Who will welcome you in Duat after what you've done?" She scoffed at Sekhmet's silence. "That's what I thought. You know where to bring him. We'll be waiting."

The pressure shifted in my ears, telling me that she'd coined off after having the last word. It was a subtle clue that often went unnoticed unless one was holding their breath the way I was.

"Pussycat," Sekhmet muttered under her breath. "I'll show her a pussycat when I make the rivers flow with blood."

A second pressure shift followed her pouting rant, this time concluding with a soft *pop*. And then we were alone in the silent darkness once again.

"Did you hear that?" Anubis asked, panic hitching his voice.

"Yeah," Bub said. "Feisty things, aren't they? Thought we were going to have a real cat fight on our hands."

"What? Not that." Anubis shook his head. "Seth's priest is already inside."

"But the rest of the cult isn't," I reminded him, wondering just how long we had before they did show up. Sekhmet would be returning, too. I couldn't decide which run-in would be worse. Sekhmet was a violent war goddess who could hold her own in a fight, but helplessly watching mortals resurrect Seth with no more authority or sway than an average ghost would be just as painful.

"We should get this search party underway before it gets much later," Bub said, clicking his flashlight on again. "Could be at it a while with a bum map."

Anubis nodded in agreement and waved for us to follow him through the east entrance of the complex wall. Inside was nothing more than a shadowy maze of rubble. The archaeologists had been busy. I couldn't tell which holes in the ground were crypt entrances and which ones were abandoned digs until we were practically on top of them.

Saul dipped his nose over the lip of a dark shaft and whimpered. The sound that echoed back made my nerves twitch.

"Well done, beastie," Anubis said, holding the scroll up for Bub to shine some light on our situation. "There are two adjoining crypts below that have been documented by the mortals, but a hidden entrance within one grants access to a tunnel network that remains undiscovered—to the general public anyway. I suspect Sekhmet has revealed this secret entrance to Seth's priest."

"Suppose she revealed a ladder, too?" Bub said, his brow puckering as he stared into the shaft.

"You see the hand and footholds there?" Anubis pointed at two parallel side walls where a series of holes had been dug all the way down. "No one wants to get stuck in a crypt that deep, believe you me. This is a holy site, not a prison for criminals."

Saul whimpered again and licked the back of my hand. I understood his concern, but there was no resolving it.

"You'll have to stay behind." I sighed and ruffled his ears.

"Here," Bub said, digging the last protein bar out of his pack. "Best to lighten our load anyway."

I unwrapped the bar and led my hound to a stretch of stone blocks within the compound. It reminded me of the foundation that had outlined Isis's chapel behind Hathor's temple, though there were no hieroglyphs etched on these stones.

"*Manto*," I said, pointing to a hidden nook behind the short wall. Saul circled the blocks and laid down slowly, eyes still focused on his reward. "Stay hidden and be quiet," I instructed, tossing him the snack bar. "We'll be back soon."

Maybe that was wishful thinking, but I sure hoped it was true. The less time we spent in damp, dark tunnels, the better.

"You know," Anubis said as Bub resecured his pack, "many divine myths involve emerging from a cave often linked to the underworlds."

I gave him a dry smile. "Well, aren't I a lucky girl."

"Goddesses first?" he offered, opening his hand at the creepy shaft.

In every way imaginable, Taposiris Magna made Dendera look like a five-star hotel. The underground passages here were not the carefully cut and artfully inscribed variety Hathor's temple boasted. No, the path to Cleopatra's tomb was little more than a hole, burrowed into the bedrock as if by a giant creature's claws and teeth. The floors were uneven and slick with moisture, and every so often one of us would misstep in a slimy puddle or bash an elbow into the jagged walls.

Anubis consulted the charred map at every turn, and at every turn I became less certain he knew where we were or where we were going. We were tired, hungry, and hopelessly lost. It was anyone's guess how long we had until sunrise, but dread had already sunk its hooks into me.

"I think I've narrowed it down to these two passages," Anubis said as we reached a new junction. "Things could get a bit dicey now, but I'm ninety percent certain we go this way." He pointed a hand down a tunnel to his left.

"And where does the other ten percent take us?" I asked.

"If I'm reading this right…" Anubis cleared his throat and looked back at the scroll. "A watery pit of vipers."

I rolled my eyes. "You sure know how to show a girl a good time."

He gave me a sheepish smile and turned the flashlight down the tunnel before resuming our journey. We didn't make it very far.

"Bloody hell!" Bub snarled as his forehead connected with a sharp rock protruding from the ceiling.

"*Shhh.*" Anubis held up a hand. "Do you hear that?"

I shot a dirty look over my shoulder at him and then turned back to Bub's injury. The cut was bleeding into his eyebrow and trailing down his cheekbone. Not a lot of blood, but enough to make a mess of his otherwise handsome face.

"First aid kit?" I whispered, nodding to my bag still slung over his shoulder. He'd insisted on my hands remaining free, since they still packed the biggest punch while we were trapped among the mortals.

"It's fine," he said, shooing me away. "Just a flesh wound."

"Listen," Anubis hissed again. He'd made the demand at least a dozen times since we'd entered the trollish labyrinth.

"We've been down here for hours," I snapped. "At this point, I don't think you're even capable of finding our way back to the surface."

"My dear Death." Anubis pressed a hand to his heart. "As the original dog father, I dare say my tracking nose is every bit as proficient as your hound's—"

A scuffling noise deep in the passage interrupted our bickering, and the flicker of a flame in a lantern sent a spike of panic through me before I remembered that Seth's cult was mortal and couldn't see us.

For now, it appeared we only had the priest to contend with. He was a tall, thin man who was forced to hunch over as he ventured through the tunnels. The smell of musky ritual incense wafted from his robes, and his skin was slick with oil. The lantern he held close to his face illuminated dark kohl eyeliner and an ankh drawn on the center of his forehead, as well as the glint of his wide smile. Tonight was clearly his eighties goth fantasies come to life.

"You see?" Anubis whispered, theatrically waving his free hand at the priest as the man paused to push aside a slab of stone sandwiched between the rough edges of the wall. Golden light spilled out of the crypt, but the priest seemed unsurprised as he ducked inside. "I have delivered you unto the tomb," Anubis announced.

I smirked at his melodramatic posture. "Lucky guess."

"Lucky?" He scoffed. "I think I deserve a bit more credit than that."

"Sorry, we're fresh out of treats." Bub snickered, then cleared his throat as the god glared at him. "I think we're all getting a bit tired and hangry. We'll resolve both dilemmas just as soon as we take care of this one," he said apologetically, though the end was in sight. It was hard not to get swept up in relief, however premature.

Anubis cocked his head in agreement and stuffed the scroll back in Bub's open pack before chasing after the priest. We stayed close behind, eager to see this through and return home. The mortal world was not for the faint of heart.

With the condition of Taposiris and its crypts, my expectations of Cleopatra's tomb had shifted drastically. I wouldn't have been shocked to find her remains in a rough-cut hole in the bedrock, wrapped in linen and without a death mask or crown to commemorate her reign.

Apollo had conquered her kingdom and stolen her talisman. Allowing a lavish burial seemed out of character for him—a few thousand years ago, anyway. He was more laid back these days, spending much of his time tending to his brewery in Olympus.

Still, I hadn't expected a gilded room hung with bronze lanterns, nor a sarcophagus set with precious stones. The walls and floor were smooth, and hieroglyphs ran in tidy rows between bas-reliefs of Isis and Serapis, similar to the illustrations in her new temple in Duat. Several trunks overflowing with bronze coins and turquoise-crusted collars rested against the far wall.

The ceiling was taller, allowing Seth's priest to rise to his full height. In the fuller light of the room, I could now see the leopard fur cloak tucked under his arm.

"Thieving scoundrel," Anubis barked in the man's face.

Of course, this earned no reaction whatsoever. We were useless among the living mortals. They disregarded us like a parent ignores a toddler having a tantrum in a grocery store aisle. Only a summoned being could appear to them or communicate in any way, unless they were an original believer.

"My book!" Anubis pointed at an open tome on a stone pulpit at the foot of Cleopatra's sarcophagus. "This donkey-faced cretin has my book!"

Again, the priest ignored the god, opting instead to lift his eyes and hands in prayer.

"Hear me, oh Son of Nut, god of the desert sands and storms, of creatures that dwell in dark waters, you whom they called Prince of the South, bringer of disease and violence, you who have been expelled from the Two Lands. Come forth and bear witness to the mortal vessel of your rebirth."

The air in the room stirred, and I held my breath, waiting to see if Seth would materialize. Though I'd been told it would take the sacrificial ritual to make it so, fear tickled my flight instincts, and my skin crawled with sickly anticipation.

The priest paused and glanced down at Anubis's open book, carefully turning a brittle sheet of papyrus. I imagined it had once been part of a scroll—or a collection of scrolls, considering the thickness of the tome.

"Blasphemy!" Anubis shrieked. "There is no verse dedicated to the cursed one put to page by my hand. He twists my words, calling on Seth in place of Osiris."

"You need not convince us," Bub said, though worry twisted his features as Anubis's mood deteriorated.

"We know he's a hack," I offered, attempting to calm the god's hysteria. "But he can't pull off the ritual without the rest of his cult, right? We still have time to figure this out."

Anubis bared his teeth at the man. "Let him figure *this* out," he snarled. His hands reached for the book, fingers curled as if to wretch the pages from its spine, but his soul matter thinned just shy of destruction.

The codex was in use, however much Anubis's spell had been butchered. It was a bridge now, caught somewhere between this side of the grave and the other, yet moored to the mortal realm by Seth's new age priest. It was protected by the same spells on the queen's sarcophagus that warned graverobbers away from her remains and treasures. Anubis was no longer the book's master.

"What? No!" He tried again, clawing at the pages. His nails scratched the stone pulpit, and to my surprise, the priest gasped at the sound.

"I feel your presence, Warrior of Ra." He stroked the head of the leopard cloak draped over his shoulder as if he thought some spark of Seth might now reside there and welcome being coddled like a domestic feline. Humans were such funny creatures. "I shall return with your faithful servants and bring you forth into the light, mighty Lord of the Red Land. Together we will take back Egypt and reign in glorious chaos."

The priest bowed in Anubis's general direction, eliciting more outrage from the god.

"Gah!" Anubis screamed, hands fisting in his hair. "Ammit will feast on your wretched heart!"

The priest then turned on his heel and marched out of the room. He seemed far more confident about the tunnels than we had, but he'd clearly had more time to explore them. I resisted the urge to follow, knowing he'd be back with the rest of his cult. Plus, Anubis was agitated enough without me questioning his ability to navigate the crypts.

We needed the peace to regroup and form a new plan anyway. But then the sound of grinding stone drew my attention to the entrance just as the slab slid back into place, the seams fading against the smooth interior wall, closing us inside.

CHAPTER TWENTY-ONE

*"Now you watch the parades and processions of hopeful
and despairing people walking outside your tomb. They are all
looking for the answer to the problem you know so well."*
—Lynette Fromme

THERE WAS JUST SOMETHING about being trapped in a tiny room with walls covered in a dead language that made my pulse kick and sent bile into the back of my throat. It was as if my body were preparing to purge the tainted beer that had followed the last time we'd found ourselves in this situation.

Bub's breath hitched with panic as his hands searched the smooth stone where the open doorway had been a moment before. "There's no handle. Why isn't there a handle on this side?"

"It's so sacrificial vessels don't get cold feet and make a run for it," Anubis said, gaze still pinned to the stolen book, though he appeared less outraged and more puzzled now. "That's not my writing. That's not my writing at all." His eyes lit with understanding, and he made a disgusted noise in the back of his throat. "So that's how she managed to lead Seth's cult here and reveal the tomb to them."

"What if we take the talisman?" I asked, glancing at Cleopatra's elaborate sarcophagus.

"*Can* we take it?" Bub cocked his head at the stone pulpit. "Or is it affected by the same enchantment that prevents us from claiming the book?"

"There's only one way to find out," Anubis said.

We circled the ornate coffin and took in the colorful likeness of the late queen. There was no massive series of golden nesting boxes like those that had encased Tut, but it was still a regal container. Turquoise, lapis lazuli, pearls, and carnelian swirled in dazzling patterns over every square inch of stone, with gold filling the narrow spaces between, and obsidian eyes dotted with stars of quartz stared up at the ceiling of the crypt.

"Isn't the pearl we're looking for split in half? These all look intact," I said, my hand hovering over the array. After the incident with the scrolls, I was hesitant to touch shiny things in tight spaces. My gaze followed that of Isis's gilded image, searching the ceiling for openings that could potentially spew sand or water, scorpions or snakes.

"Perhaps it's inside?" Bub suggested. My nose scrunched at the idea. I was no stranger to the dead, but I did prefer fresher harvests.

Anubis shook his head. "Something is not right here." He pointed out a pattern in the golden border that lined the rim of the sarcophagus lid. It had seemed purely decorative at first glance, but upon closer inspection, I noticed the tiny hieroglyphs encased in oval cartouches. "Queen of Heaven, Cosmic Mother, Star of the Sea… These are all names she shares with other goddesses."

"And only the celestial ones, I take it?" Bub said.

I looked up at the wall behind the head of the sarcophagus. The writing was smaller in scale here than it had been inside the temple at Dendera, and there were fewer illustrations spaced between the rows of text.

"What does it say?" I asked as Anubis followed my gaze to the lengthy scripture.

"That you should settle in because this could take a while." He sighed and migrated to the corner of the room where the engravings began. One hand followed the path of his pensive gaze, trailing from ceiling to floor, then floor to ceiling as he read under his breath. I couldn't understand the language he spoke, but I expected he would translate whatever he deemed relevant and useful.

Bub and I watched, quietly waiting, covering our occasional yawns. It was late, and I was so very tired. I could feel my body begging to give it up and let sleep take over. Not that my accelerating heart rate would allow anything even remotely resembling sleep. And though my stomach still ached from trying to turn itself inside out that morning, I would have traded a kidney for a fat, juicy ribeye and one of Rupert's thrice-baked potatoes. If I never saw another protein bar again, it would be too soon.

"I think this is a decoy tomb," Anubis finally announced. He tapped a finger on a cartouche squeezed in between the hieroglyphs. "This title here doesn't reference the throne, one of the key elements of Isis's identity. This cannot be Cleopatra's final resting place."

"You mean we came all this way for nothing?" I propped my hands on my hips and glared at him. "Does it say where the hell the real tomb is?"

"Sort of. Maybe." Anubis's face flushed as he went back and reread a section before moving further down the wall.

"Either it does or it doesn't," I said through clenched teeth. Bub's disheartened sigh stoked my guilt, and I turned to him, not waiting for the god's answer. "I'm so sorry I dragged you into this. I should have listened in Cairo. We could be at a hospital right now, moments from salvation, and instead we're trapped in a phony tomb, moments from being discovered by a murderous goddess."

"At least we're together." Bub gave me a small smile. "And if this is the wrong tomb, surely that means there's no talisman for Seth's cult to complete their ritual."

"But Sekhmet has seen the scroll," Anubis interjected. "She would not have led the priest to this room otherwise. Which means the talisman must be here *somewhere*."

I stared down at the sarcophagus, wondering if we'd be digging through some crusty remains after all. It seemed rather pointless, considering the talisman was likely locked in the same magical limbo as Anubis's Book of Eternal Breath.

"Listen to this," the god said, reading from the wall. "The keys lie in her child's eyes. One of night, soft and blue. The other red, and burning true. They hold court where towns, streets, and rivers are found, but not a soul."

"More riddles?" I scoffed, though my eyes searched the tomb, trying to make sense of it all.

"The first part is clearly in reference to the sun and moon, yes?" Bub said.

"Or perhaps a metaphor for them." Anubis frowned. "Cleopatra and Mark Antony had twins, Alexander Helios and Cleopatra Selene. But the Ptolemaic dynasty fell before either was of age to rule. The court mentioned here… it makes no sense."

"What are these?" I asked, pointing out two convex circles that stood out among the symbols on the wall, roughly three feet between them. They seemed out of place with the few other illustrations pushing outward in bas-relief fashion, as if they'd been carved into the wall backwards. "What does it say here between them?" I fingered the engravings, annoyed that I couldn't read the ancient language.

"The path you seek, you have already found," Anubis recited, his brow creasing deeper with every word. "Lay the eyes upon the sky, and the Queen of Heaven shall be revealed."

"Already found?" I sucked in a shallow breath and grabbed the end of the map scroll sticking out of Bub's pack. I shook it at Anubis. "This is the only *path* we've found so far. And given its condition, if the answer was here, I'm guessing we're screwed."

The god's face crumpled. He hadn't admitted it, but it was obvious he'd bluffed his way through the tunnels with what little of the papyrus had survived the Giza incident.

"Why eyes?" Bub asked. "What do eyes have to do with the sun and the moon?"

Anubis shrank away from my scorn, eager for the distraction. "The sun and moon were the eyes of Ra. When Isis learned his true name, she used it to claim the sun and moon for Horus."

"So would these be stars then?" Bub's hand moved across the stone wall, pointing out several marks randomly placed between the hieroglyphs. "Are we looking at a sky here?"

"Could be," Anubis said. "Though these don't appear to form any actual constellations."

I unrolled the charred map and held it up for comparison. Maybe I'd get lucky and something would pop out at me, like a big red arrow I'd somehow missed the last dozen times I'd inspected the ruined page.

Anubis sighed. "Trust me, you won't find any new towns, streets, or rivers there."

"You're probably right." I frowned and blinked down at the map anyway. "But you know what else I'm not finding? *Souls.*"

I closed the scroll and tilted it to have a look at the end cap. It was smeared with soot, but I could still see the carnelian stone beneath. The setting in the leather was already loose from the abuse it had endured, and it took nothing to pry it free with a carefully placed fingernail.

"What are you doing?" Anubis snapped. He took the scroll from me, but I kept the cap and used the end of my blouse to wipe it clean.

"Lay the eyes upon the sky…" I held up the red-orange stone, positioning it over the first indention. They were roughly the same size, and when I touched it to the wall, a metallic echo filled the room as it snapped into place.

Anubis's eyes lit with understanding. "That's it," he rasped, removing the lapis lazuli end from the scroll. He gave it a quick polish on his stained tunic and pressed it into the remaining frame. Another sharp sound resonated through the room, and then the twin stones flared to life, glowing brighter as the wall between them split apart.

Sandy debris sifted down from the ceiling, and Bub reached for my arm, pulling me back a step as the tomb trembled. I felt the vibrations in the floor, through the soles of my boots. It rattled my bones and set my nerves on fire, filling me with a giddy, nauseating thrill.

Was the crypt on the verge of collapse, or were we on the verge of discovery? Who could say for certain?

After a moment that felt like an eternity, the world grew still again, and the break in the wall revealed its purpose. Two doors, one cut around each stone, had opened inwardly to reveal a secret room.

It was a smaller, less assuming space, illuminated by nothing more than the glow of the twin stones. Two coffins made of smooth stone rested side-by-side with cartouches marking the lids of each. There were no precious stones or elaborate paintings. Even the walls were bare, save for a thick outline that mirrored the entrance. It reminded me of the magical exit we'd used to escape the scroll room at Dendera.

"This one," Anubis said, pointing out the symbols engraved on the second coffin. "She's in here." He handed off the scroll to me and waved for Bub to take

the foot of the lid. They pushed on opposite sides, sliding the heavy stone diagonally across the rim of the box
until an opening appeared at the head.

The smell of old leather and wax tinged the air, and
something sour like vinegar or rotten fruit. The dressings
wrapped around the queen were surprisingly white and
loose enough that it took little effort to part the material
and expose her sunken face. Though I'd expected to find
gray-green flesh like that of her predecessors in the museum, she was covered in gold. It crinkled over her
cheeks and around her eyes, where the fat and muscle
had rotted away beneath her skin. Still, there was something oddly beautiful about her.

Anubis reached inside the coffin and came away with
a handful of leather-wrapped scrolls. Their end caps
were made of polished wood rather than gemstones, but
the wax seals bore a striking resemblance to the ones
used on the scrolls from Dendera. Anubis held one up
to read a title scrawled into the leather cover.

"Creed of the Inimitable Livers," he said, grinning
dryly. "For as much as she loved to study languages and
politics, she was also fond of her drinking club and the
shenanigans they got up to."

He reached deeper, into the portion of the stone box
still hidden beneath the lid, and found a sheaf of loose
papyrus, bottles of dried ink, and box of reed quills. Bub,
who was still at the foot of the coffin, withdrew several

bottles of wine and what looked to be perfume. But no pearls.

"I don't see a talisman," I said, flipping through the papyrus pages as if Cleopatra's cult would have hidden it so carelessly among her remains after the lengths they'd gone to, to hide her tomb.

"I'm sure there's a clue in here somewhere," Anubis said, nudging the gilded skeleton aside to rut around for more afterlife loot. But there was nothing more to be discovered.

"Do we have enough time to go through all of this?" I asked, squinting at the dainty handwriting scrawled on the loose pages. It was more recognizable to me than the hieroglyphs, perhaps Greek, though I still couldn't read it.

Anubis shook his head. "These scrolls belonged to Cleopatra and would have been sealed long before she and Antony were moved here. And Isis's cult would have placed too much value on the love letters to alter them."

"What about this?" Bub asked, joining us at the head of the coffin. He pressed a finger to the thick lip of the coffin where a line of shallow text had been engraved. It was nearly invisible in the soft light coming from the stones.

"Good eye," Anubis said. He hunched over to take a closer look and frowned. "Something about a heart and... bone. It's quite faint."

"Here." I opened one of the ink bottles and snatched the last of our water from Bub's pack, using as little as possible to wet my finger. Then I dipped it in the ink dust and gave it a swirl. The murky, watercolor consistency would do the trick. I smeared it over the line of text, filling the engravings to reveal the symbols in sharper contrast against the pale stone.

Anubis tried again with better success. "Her mortal heart resides in a cave of bone where lovers breathe unspoken vows."

I rolled my eyes. "I hate these damn riddles."

"Really?" Bub said, a small grin quirking his lips. "I think I'm finally getting the hang of them. Check her mouth, pet."

Thankfully, Anubis beat me to it. He pried her jaw open, scattering flakes of gold over the gauzy wrappings. Among Cleopatra's dingy teeth, two pearly whites stood out, fashioned in place of her canines. Their extended length made her look like a vampire with rounded-off fangs.

"Oh, sure." I snorted. "Don't tamper with the love poems, but post-mortem dentistry? No problem."

"You have to admit, it's a good hiding place," Bub said. "Who would think to go digging around in the mouth of a mummy?"

Anubis pinched one of the pearl teeth and tried to twist it free, but it refused to budge, even as Cleopatra's skull rocked from side to side. He glanced up at us. "You didn't happen to pack a set of pliers, did you?"

"Seriously, mate?" Bub hitched a brow in amused annoyance. "I didn't even pack enough underwear."

"It's not like we can make off with the talisman anyway," I said. "We're stuck here until that priest comes back, likely with the cult and Sekhmet in tow."

"That's a fair point," Anubis said, picking up the jar of rehydrated ink I'd left on the lid of the coffin. He flipped over one of the papyrus love letters, revealing a blank backside, and then glanced behind us at the false door drawn on the tomb wall. I could almost see the wheels turning in his head as he grabbed one of the reed quills and used the end to stir the crusty ink.

"What are you doing?" Bub asked.

"Something I haven't done for a very long time."

"Is there anything we can do to help?" I offered.

Anubis pressed the reed to the page and began writing. "Pray it works."

CHAPTER TWENTY-TWO

"The boundaries which divide Life from Death
are at best shadowy and vague. Who shall say
where the one ends, and where the other begins?"
—Edgar Allan Poe

EVEN THOUGH CLEOPATRA had been a mortal vessel of Isis, and the cult that had hidden her here at Taposiris Magna was no more, I still felt compelled to treat her tomb and effects with respect. The scrolls and wine and perfume all went back exactly where we'd found them. I had a feeling they wouldn't remain that way for long, but what Seth's cult did was beyond my control. At least my conscience was clear.

No mummy curses for me, thank you.

Of course, I still felt some obligation for opening the secret tomb in the first place. But we couldn't exactly close up the doors and remove the stones without the talisman in hand. We had just returned to the task of attempting to dislodge the queen's pearly whites when our time finally ran out.

The sound of stone grinding on stone set my teeth on edge, and a tremor of dread crawled up my spine. Anubis pulled the gauze dressing up to hide Cleopatra's mouth, and we all turned toward the hidden entrance as the priest stepped inside, lantern held high.

The man's kohl-streaked face creased with equal parts elation and skepticism. He squinted into every corner of the room, not seeing us though clearly taking note of the open coffin. This was all new, and he was clearly trying to decide if it was a rival cult or divine intervention. He inched closer, eyes swelling as he took in the golden face of the mummy.

"Is everything in place, Samir?" a man called to him from the faux tomb.

"Yes, yes," the priest shouted back, turning away. "Close the door. Let us begin."

I blew out a tense breath, only to suck in another as Sekhmet appeared, filling the doorway. She was draped in a black robe, matching the cult moving around in the bejeweled room behind her, though the red skirt stretched an inch past the hem. The golden cobra cuffs had been moved to the outsides of her sleeves, and a matching uraeus—a circlet crown with an erect cobra— perched on her head.

"Well, well." she purred. "Did the mice play while the cat was away?"

"We have the talisman," Anubis said, which was only half true, but I wasn't about to point that out.

"Doesn't matter." Sekhmet shrugged. "Without a coin, you're not going anywhere. And so long as the talisman is within this tomb, it will enable Seth's rebirth. Why do you think I led his cult here?"

"Yes, I noticed your desecration of my sacred book." Anubis's upper lip curled with distaste.

The sound of the stone slab door closing in the other room removed any thoughts I might've had of making a run for it. Tucking tail wasn't part of the plan, no matter how twitchy my flight instincts were. Sekhmet's formal garb made Seth's arrival feel too imminent, and I didn't have a hellcat to mow her over with this time. Her feline eyes shifted from Anubis to me, and my heart trembled at her predatory poise.

"I dare say, I am surprised your tagalongs made it this far," she said. "How much coin did dear Isis promise you?"

"I'm not doing this for the coin," I blurted. Even shaking in my boots, I had my pride.

"That's right," Sekhmet cooed. "I'd almost forgotten. You want to be a goddess when you grow up." She chuckled and then clicked her tongue. "Trust me, reaper. The only reason Isis would ever support your campaign for deity status is if she thought you inferior and harmless. Why do you think I'm here instead of Hathor?"

"If you wanted your mother form back, why didn't you use the talisman for that instead of resurrecting Seth?" I asked. Not that she needed any more bad ideas, but a fun-loving party goddess who liked booze and babies seemed by far the lesser of two evils.

"Why would I want to be Hathor when Seth and his cult can restore my former glory as a goddess of warfare and pestilence?" She cackled at my horrified surprise and took a step inside the tomb, her hand resting on the foot of Cleopatra's coffin. "I'm but a shadow of what I once was. Just as you're but a shadow of Death, an echo of a primordial power you've allowed others to dilute with their jealousy and fear. You could be so much more, if only—"

Voices filtered in from the decoy tomb, low and rhythmic. And then the priest began his part, clumsily stumbling over the ancient language in Anubis's book. The ritual was beginning.

"If only what?" I asked Sekhmet, snagging her attention again. "Don't tell me you're inviting me to join your exclusive bad guy club." I pressed a hand to my chest and batted my lashes. "I don't know what to say. This is all so sudden."

She smirked and dropped her gaze to Cleopatra's linen-wrapped remains. "You could be so much more," she repeated, "if only I didn't intend to feast on your flesh and bathe in your blood."

My throat went dry. I tried to swallow, but without moisture, it was a slow recovery. Slow enough that she heard the priest in the next room.

"Fumbling fool," she hissed, turning on her heel to stalk out of the tomb. "You're saying it all wrong!"

"We need to get the talisman out, now," Anubis whispered through clenched teeth. "We have but moments to spare."

Bub yanked the cloth down from Cleopatra's face and braced a hand on either side of her golden skull while Anubis pinched and pulled at her pearl fangs to no effect. I watched helplessly in between peeking past the stone doors to keep an eye on Sekhmet.

The goddess paced behind the priest, screaming profanities at him for his ineptness. Of course, he couldn't hear her any more than he had heard Anubis earlier. She'd lured the cult here by altering the Book of Eternal Breath, adding details about the tomb and a blasphemous, Frankenstein ritual that combined Isis's mortal vessel spell with Osiris's resurrection spell and aimed it at the creep supreme of their pantheon.

But two could play that game.

Realization finally dawned on Sekhmet when the priest reached the part of Anubis's new and improved ritual that required him to torch the book and the leopard cloak. He held up his oil lantern and hesitated, almost as if he could hear the unhinged goddess shrieking in his face. Then he poured the burning oil over the papyrus codex and set it ablaze with the lantern's flame.

The other members of the cult gasped. They clearly hadn't been expecting such a sacrifice. Their hysteria only escalated when the priest laid the leopard cloak over the blazing pulpit. The dry fur caught fire instantly, filling the room with smoke, and I lost sight of Sekhmet.

I coughed and waved a hand in front of my face as the fumes worked their way inside the smaller tomb. The stone doors were heavy, but I tried to push one closed anyway. Until Sekhmet's hands curled around my throat.

"You fools!" she screamed. "You've ruined everything."

My hands instinctively went to her wrists as she backed me further inside the room. It only took three steps before my hip rammed into Antony's coffin. Sekhmet lifted me onto my toes, and my gurgled protest died as she slammed my back onto the stone lid.

"This isn't over," she snarled, pressing her face in close to mine, "but you are."

Her nose began to flatten, and fur sprouted from her eyebrows, circling her eyes before spreading across her forehead and down her cheeks. The lioness was emerging, just as it had in Dendera—right before she breathed flames into the sand font in the scroll room.

My first thought was to fight fire with fire. But it was a little hard to recite Latin spells with my throat crushed in her furry, clawed soon-to-be murder mitts. Especially with my vision going spotty from the lack of oxygen.

Bub's backpack sailed through the air, cracking the goddess in the side of the head. Without his Eternity-side powers or any weapons, his options were limited. The little old lady with a brick in her purse method seemed to piss Sekhmet off more than it incapacitated her. Still, it turned her attention away long enough for me to catch my breath. I was going to need it.

Sekhmet pounced on my demon, shoving him to the floor between the two coffins. She pressed a knee into his chest and pinned his arms over his head. With her lion muzzle so close, he was forced to close his eyes against the smoke curling from her blackened nostrils. Her jaws parted, and my world came into sharp, heart-stopping focus.

Fire blossomed in my chest and spread down my arms. It wasn't the kind that scorched my fingertips when I spouted the Latin fire spell. This was the innate power that marked me as other. A dark, accidental inheritance from my late *godfather.*

I didn't remember rising from Antony's coffin or crossing the room. But somehow, I found myself standing beside Sekhmet, one glowing, burning hand wrapped around the back of her neck. Her mouth hung open, inches from Bub's sweat-slick face, but her gaze had turned to me. Even at such a sharp angle, I saw her fear. I *tasted* it.

"I could melt his flesh from the bone in the blink of an eye," she warned, though her words quivered.

"And I could siphon your soul matter to make him whole again," I said flatly. I'd meant it as a bluff, but something in my core wrapped around the threat, whispering like so many voices that I'd heard once before. I *had* brought people back from the dead—Bub included. Though I'd thought that ability linked to the throne power which I'd released into the sea.

Or had I? Could I have been wrong? Was that something I was still capable of?

I'd said so with enough authority to give Sekhmet pause.

My grip tightened on the back of her neck, and I felt my fingers warm, preparing to melt through her flesh. She rasped out a startled breath and released Bub's arms, slowly leaning away from him as I pulled her upright and then to her feet.

"What are you?" she whispered, her voice rasping with uncertainty.

"Just a shadow of Death, pussycat." My grin felt tight and unnatural across my face, as if it were struggling against my tightly wound nerves. I was a compressed coil, waiting for release.

Sekhmet's pulse throbbed through her flesh, beating like a trapped bird against my palm. I focused on it, waiting to see if she'd lash out or try to run. That would be all the catalyst I needed. There was no off switch once things escalated this far. The power was a trap waiting to spring, and I had little control over it. It washed over me in waves of sick elation, promising a heady rush of power if Sekhmet would so much as breathe wrong.

Some twisted part of me wished she would.

"Lana?" Anubis said, easing into my peripheral vision. His face creased with some strange emotion I'd not seen in him before. Was that fear? Concern? "Please, don't," he begged. "Hathor is still in there. Isis will see to it that Sekhmet is properly punished."

The uproar in the decoy tomb was beginning to fade as the cult members opened the door into the tunnel and abandoned the ritual. Thankfully, they'd made it far enough to trigger the false door inside the real tomb. A glowing blue light filled the outline etched into the stone. It pulsed with increasing frequency as if counting down how long we had to make our escape.

I stared at it over Sekhmet's shoulder, frozen in place by the searing power coursing through my veins and the dread knotting in my guts.

Bub grabbed the side of Cleopatra's coffin and dragged himself up off the floor. His worried face mirrored Anubis's, though he looked less surprised. He was well aware of what I could do when pushed to my limits.

"It's time to go home, pet," he said, cocking his head at the glowing doorway. He eased a step closer and placed his hand over my forearm, gently so as not to prompt a soul-sucking disaster.

The fire in me tapered as it had outside the temple walls. My aversion to hurting him was stronger than my desire for vengeance. The feeling that inspired was convoluted, shifting from resentment to relief as my senses came back to me.

I pushed Sekhmet toward Anubis, silently surrendering her to his custody. Her shoulders sagged as he took her by the arms, and a shuddering sob slipped past her lips. They were human again, her face having shifted back at some point during the deadlock with my grim tendency. Her gaze dropped to the floor as if she were too afraid or ashamed to look at any of us.

I supposed *I* was a bit embarrassed, too. Though I pushed it aside when the light around the bespelled door began flashing faster. The sound of the slab door sliding shut in the next room sent my panic into overdrive.

"We're out of time," Bub said, tugging my arm.

"The talisman—" Anubis ground his teeth and shot a desperate glance back at Cleopatra's gaping mouth.

"There's more than one way to skin a cat." I pulled away from Bub and reached both hands into the coffin, placing one on either side of the queen's skull. With a sharp *snap, crackle, pop*, the head was free of its body.

Both Bub and Anubis made a face as I lifted it for them to see.

"Gotta think outside the box, boys," I said, tucking the skull under one arm before heading for the glowing doorway. "Let's get the hell out of here."

CHAPTER TWENTY-THREE

*"At the end of the day, we can endure
much more than we think we can."*
—*Frida Kahlo*

BEFORE THE CELTIC GOD Cernunnos revolutionized spectral travel and launched a new era of technological advancement across the afterlives by opening Bank of Eternity and introducing his mysterious coins, getting to and from the mortal realm was an entirely different ordeal.

There were various natural passages like Hecate's Grove in Tartarus, the secret hill entrances to Faerie, and hellmouths aplenty. But there were also a few ancient gateways, tucked away in remote caves. All these passages were sealed off once Cern's coins were adopted by the immortal masses. The order came from Grim, of course, and was carried out via the Throne of Eternity he still controlled through Khadija.

Still, there were some gateways even Death himself could not command. Namely, those crafted by original believers and installed in the mortal realm. Khadija could manipulate the soul matter in Eternity, but her powers were confined to this side of the grave.

These false doors drawn on temple walls became less problematic as the pagan faiths fell out of favor and new religions rose up to replace them. Thankfully, disuse had no bearing on their functionality.

The one we passed through in Cleopatra's tomb spit us out inside Isis's new temple in Duat. Bub cracked his head on a scaffolding bar. Anubis ducked but managed to trip over a crossbeam, and I narrowly missed a collision with Sekhmet as she was thrust into the room behind me, spilling across the floor.

"By the dog," Isis swore, taking us in with wide eyes from across the room. She'd traded her queenly party garb for a simple white gown, making her look more like a temple maiden. One hand was frozen in the air, finger pointing at a bas-relief in the works.

The sculptor, perched atop another tower of scaffolding, held her chisel dangerously close to the stone nose of some god or another. Her attention had shifted to us as well, and she wobbled on the edge of her seat.

"We'll have to reschedule for another time," Isis said, dismissing the sculptor. "Leave us."

The woman tucked her tools in a bucket and hurried down the ladder. She shot us one last sideways glance before exiting through the front entrance I'd passed through during the party just days before. It felt as if I'd been dragged through the bowels of Hell to get back here.

"Do you have it?" Isis asked as soon as the sculptor was gone.

Do you have it? My mind reeled at her indifference to our bruised and bloodied condition.

"We do," Anubis answered before I could give her a piece of my mind. "No thanks to Sekhmet," he added, giving the goddess kneeling on the floor a pointed stare. "She rallied Seth's cult, stole a sacred text, and attempted to use your talisman to resurrect him."

Isis sighed and gazed down at the cowering goddess. "Vengeful daughter of Ra, your time has come." She touched Sekhmet's head with more tenderness than I expected, gently removing the cobra crown and handing it to Anubis. "You served well in the war, and I meant to reward your loyalty by allowing you to remain in place of Hathor," Isis said.

"You meant to eliminate your competition and hoard favor with Horus," Sekhmet replied, turning a scathing glare up at Isis.

"Maybe some part of that is true, as well," Isis admitted. "But now we both have consequences to face for our actions. We will shoulder them together." She looked to Anubis. "The talisman, my faithful son," she requested.

I stepped forward instead, depositing the golden skull in her outstretched hand. "The teeth," I said, pointing out the pearl tips inside Cleopatra's mouth. "We couldn't get them out. Your cult must have used super glue or—"

"I'll see to you momentarily." Isis's eyes narrowed, and the skin between her brows pinched as she took a closer look at me. I couldn't quite tell if her statement was a threat or a polite address to take a number, as if I were in line at the DMV.

She rotated the skull in her hands and focused her sharp eyes on the pearl halves. I couldn't help but feel a pinch of embarrassment as she grasped one and gave it a single twist, breaking it free from the socket. The other detached with equal ease, drawing an astonished gasp from me.

Bub tilted his chin over my shoulder and angled his mouth toward my ear. "I'm sure we loosened it for her," he said.

Anubis snorted, but his smile died as Isis's gaze flicked up again. She gave him the skull and palmed the pearl halves in one hand, returning her other to Sekhmet's head.

Sekhmet's eyes filled with panic, but the animosity was still there, too. "I am only one of many who serve the lion-hearted goddess who came before. She is rising, and when she does, she will come for you." Sekhmet sneered at Anubis, Bub, and me. "She'll come for *all* of you."

"Who? Your Sumerian friend?" I smirked at her surprise. I was no detective, but her blatant attempt to stall was so painfully obvious.

"Enough." Isis closed her eyes, and light spilled around her closed fist, leaking from between her fingers. It ran through her arm and across her chest before stretching all the way to her opposite hand where it rested atop Sekhmet's head. There the light left Isis and spilled over the other goddess, changing in color from white to a fiery orange, then bluish green.

And then *Sekhmet* changed.

Her braids unfurled, and fluted cow ears slipped through her dark hair. Likewise, her facial features relaxed into softer angles, and the black robe fell away, revealing a red dress similar to the white one Isis wore. The goddess's eyes fluttered open.

"Arise, Mistress of Dendera, goddess of song and dance," Isis said, cupping Hathor's cheek. "Tonight, we celebrate your return."

As if summoned by the goddess's arrival, attendants in gold-trimmed robes appeared. They surrounded Hathor and led her away. Isis stared after them. For a moment, I thought she might follow, but then another servant appeared with a wooden box. She bowed and handed it to the goddess before disappearing again.

"For you," Isis said, offering me a faint smile. She opened the lid of the box and withdrew a black cord hung with a silver ankh. "A token of our new partnership, from one goddess to another."

I bent forward, allowing her to place the necklace over my head and ignoring the way her nose crinkled in disgust. I didn't blame her. We'd been stinking up a storm since the vomit fest in Dendera.

"It's so… shiny." The pendant was a bit out of place against my gritty, sand-dusted shirt, but I admired it anyway. At least until Isis made to leave. "I'm still getting paid, right?" I blurted. "I mean, jewelry is nice and all, but—"

"Come on." Anubis took my elbow and steered me toward the exit, waving for Bub to follow. "I'll have Horus cut you a check," he said, cackling nervously at Isis's obvious annoyance.

I made a face at his suggestion. "Can't you just drop it in the mail and spot us a coin for now?"

"Sure." He snorted. "I suppose you've dealt with enough prima deities for one weekend."

"For one lifetime," Bub muttered under his breath, linking his arm with mine on the opposite side from Anubis. We looked like we were off to see a wizard.

"I need food, a bath, and sleep, in that specific order, immediately," my demon announced, planning out our entire day. "After you call in sick to work, of course."

"First things first," I said, assessing my own list of priorities. "We have a very good boy waiting for us back in Egypt."

Despite our mortal detour to collect Saul, we made it home to Tartarus in a matter of minutes after leaving Duat. *Oh*, how I'd missed coin travel. If I'd been the religious type, I would have built a shrine to praise Cern's brilliance. And now that I knew Winston's coin was truly defunct, I'd be swapping it out for a fully loaded one to keep stashed in my boot heel from here on out.

Rupert wrenched open the front door with a gasp. "Lucifer's busted halo," he swore, taking a step back as we entered the manor in all our filthy glory. "Sh-should I call for Meng Po?"

"No, no." Bub shook his head and paused to yawn. "We'll be fine, but we could do with a bit of breakfast."

"Full spread brunch," I amended. "Buffet style. Pretend you're feeding a legion."

"Right away," Rupert said, rushing off toward the kitchen. Saul trailed after him with a wag in his tail. He was grubby too, but I didn't have the heart to banish him to the backyard. We were all smelly. At least he wasn't coated in sulfur. If I was lucky, I'd be able to squeeze him in for a bath at Hades' Hound House soon.

I'd requested Monday off after Bub and I had agreed to track down Isis's talisman. Which, if my math was correct, meant I was due back at work tomorrow. *Ugh.*

"I should call work and see if I can extend my time off by another day," I said, eyeing the desk phone through Bub's open office door. "Then the mobile hub in Limbo to order us each a new cell phone."

"It can wait until we've eaten something." Bub squeezed my shoulders and tugged me away from the office. He pulled me in for a tight, stinky hug and rested his chin on top of my head. "I haven't had a weekend run me that ragged on the mortal side since the Spanish Inquisition."

"The good old days?" I chuckled.

"Hardly," he said. "But I don't remember them ever leaving me so thirsty. I swear, I could drink a bathtub full of water."

"Just not the bathtub of water we'll be soaking in soon," I said, scrunching my nose. "Actually, we should probably shower *before* taking the bath."

"I was thinking shower, nap, and then bath," he countered. "Otherwise, we're liable to fall asleep and drown in the tub."

"Good point." I yawned and then pressed a kiss to his scruffy cheek as he reached to close the front door. A happy yip sounded from outside before the latch clicked, and he yanked it back open again.

Coreen bound up the front walk and bolted into the foyer, tongue lolling with glee. Anubis appeared soon after. His hair was wet, and he was in a fresh shirt and pants.

"Reunited, safe and sound," he said, then he tilted his nose in the air. "Is that bacon and coffee I smell?" He stepped inside without an invitation. I guessed we were beyond formalities now. Friends who got drugged and mugged in the desert together stayed together—and shared snacks, apparently.

"Help yourself," Bub said dryly.

"Much obliged." Anubis touched the brim of an invisible hat, either oblivious or willfully ignoring my demon's sarcasm, and the two of them headed for the kitchen. Coreen sat patiently at my feet. Her innocent eyes turned up to me, and she licked her muzzle, waiting for my command.

"Oh, *now* you wanna be a good dog?" I scoffed. But all she seemed to hear was *good dog*, and her ears perked cluelessly at the assumed praise. I sighed and rolled my eyes. "Go eat, *slut*."

She pressed her nose to the back of my hand and trotted off in search of Cerberus Chow.

Rupert knew his way around a kitchen. It had taken him some months to master Bub's favorite recipes, but he'd welcomed the challenge. In my opinion, there were a few he'd even made improvements to—something Bub considered blasphemy on my part.

My demon still missed Jack, and though he was warmer toward Rupert, I knew he'd give our new butler the boot if Jack ever so much as hinted that he wanted his job back. Bub's loyalty ran deep—and so did his guilt. We were a lot alike in that regard. I had a feeling I'd be apologizing for this weekend for years to come, even if it did earn him consort status.

After we had our fill of bacon, eggs, waffles, and an assortment of fruity pastries, we said our goodbyes to Anubis. Then I tasked Rupert with fetching our new phones while Bub and I showered and napped away the afternoon. It was nearly time for dinner before we rose again.

While Rupert finished preparing the sides to go with the steaks I'd requested, Bub called Asmodeus with a last-minute invitation to join us, and I checked my missed messages out on the back patio. There were five, which seemed excessive, but to be fair, I'd been MIA all weekend. I hit play, hoping to get through them before Rupert served up dinner.

"*First message*," the machine lady announced. "Lana, it's Jenni." A message from the president of Reapers Inc.

was a rarity, even if we had been roommates and friends once upon a time. And, of course, the honor never came with good news. "Your surprise cameo at Isis's party in Duat is all over GraveSpace, and now the council is breathing down my neck." I could almost hear her teeth grinding through the phone. "We need to talk. Soon."

Well, *that* was going to be a fun conversation.

"*Next message*," machine lady continued, serving up a less threatening and more concerned message from Kevin, fishing for an answer as to why I hadn't been home when he'd picked up the helljacks from Rupert.

"Ask if she needs any help," Eliza's muted voice layered behind his before he repeated her suggestion.

The third message circled back to vague threats with a check-in from Tasha. "Just wanted to remind you about our little *deal*," she cooed. "My Hellagio interview is this Friday. I'm putting you down as a reference on my resume."

As the *only* reference, I was sure. I couldn't think of anyone else who'd vouch for her.

It was my teeth doing the grinding this time. I wanted to hate Tasha, but hearing her voice still stoked my guilt. And my pity. However awful she'd been, I couldn't shake feeling at least partially responsible for her situation. *Her situation that now included being relatively wealthy.*

That she was already job hunting still struck me as odd. Sure, it was fiscally smart to keep working—especially when one was immortal. But she wasn't wasting any time. Maybe she was lonely. The thought had occurred to me before, but now it was the only one that made sense. And it twisted like a worm in my stomach as I tried my damnedest not to feel sorry for her.

Maybe I'd just warn Asmodeus to keep an eye on her and not give her access to any money room at his casino. After all, if she was working a legitimate job, that gave her less time to get into trouble or *cause* trouble for me.

The last message was from Cordelia. "Your face is all over the news! The council has called a meeting over it," she squealed, sounding far more delighted about it than Jenni had. "This is it, Lana. You're finally working your way up the ladder. You'll be the *official* patron goddess of the Woke Souls in no time. Everyone is eager to celebrate this victory with you. Come see us again as soon as you're able."

An invitation to the isles always filled me with nervous excitement. Strange and wonderful things happened there, things I couldn't explain but somehow felt tied to, as if the events were unraveling from my dreams while my eyes were wide open.

I so desperately wanted to believe in the people there who claimed to be mine. But, as always, I remained

grounded by my doubts. I could see only one way to resolve that dilemma.

"Let's get it while it's hot, pet," Bub called from the
back door, hesitating when he noticed my brooding
frown. "What is it? Is everything all right, my lover goddess?"

"I've come to a decision," I said.

"Oh? What's that?" He stepped out to join me, and
I wrapped my arms around his waist.

"That I won't be visiting the isles again without my
consort."

He blinked in surprise. "You're sure you want to give
them an ultimatum so soon?"

"Either they want a goddess, or they don't." I
shrugged. "If that's what I am to them—if that's what
they expect me to become—then I want the rights a goddess is due. And that begins with recognizing my chosen
consort. Otherwise, I'm just a sock puppet deity to them.
If that's all they want, they can name their woods and
lagoons after someone else—"

Bub cut me off with a kiss, covering my mouth with
his in a wet, minty, moan-worthy lip lock. His forked
tongue flicked mine, and he grinned as he pulled away.

"I'm flattered, truly," he said, pausing to steal more
kisses. "But if you'd really like to give this devil his due,
I have an opening in my schedule this evening, between
dinner and that bath you promised."

"I requested another day off," I reminded him. "Your schedule better be wide open tomorrow, too. If you plan on worshipping me as your lover goddess, I expect it will take all day."

"All day…" he echoed, his eager mouth moving down my jaw and to my neck. "All night… Till the end of time…"

"Uh, er—" Rupert sputtered from the back door.

"Yes?" Bub groaned before remembering why he'd come outside in the first place. "Oh, right. Dinner."

"Mr. Asmodeus has arrived," Rupert said, touching a gloved hand to his horn to better hide his flushed face.

"Let him know we'll be right there," Bub said, dismissing the mortified demon. "Quite the prude for a fiend of Hell, isn't he?"

"I think it's refreshing, and kind of adorable," I admitted as he took me by the hand and led me inside.

"You would," he teased, following it with a click of his tongue. "Lana Harvey, goddess of atheist ghosts and goody-goody demons—"

"An upgrade from confusion and humility, at least. I'll take it."

"—and queen of my heart," he added with a tender smile that I mirrored.

"I'll definitely take that."

My heart felt lighter in spite of all the uncertainty the future held. There were big changes on the horizon, but first there would be steak and thrice-baked potatoes and chocolate soufflé.

We cut through the living room on our way to the kitchen, where Coreen and Saul played tug-of-war with a knotted rope toy. Their bellies bulged with kibble and breakfast leftovers. Rupert had taken my legion-sized request to heart. Before long, Coreen's belly would be bulging with much more than leftovers.

Yes, there were *big* changes underway.

Some would cost us a small fortune in antique furniture. Others would surely lead to a political battle of wills. The rest was yet to be seen.

But with the Lord of the Flies at my side, what did I have to fear? What storm couldn't I weather with my demon consort's heart warming mine?

ACKNOWLEDGMENTS

My core team hasn't really changed all that much throughout the years. I know that must make these acknowledgments seem awfully repetitive, but it's really a wonderful feeling. It can be hard finding the right people—in all areas of life. I know how lucky I am to have found my people early on and to still be working with them today.

Special thanks to: my husband Paul, who endures my plot and research ramblings and is always first to proofread everything I write; my son Xavier who understands when I have to put in the long hours and smothers me with much-needed hugs and kisses whenever I take breaks; my critique group the Four Horsemen of the Bookocalypse whose kindness and support goes above and beyond; THE Professor George Shelley, who may be retired but will always hold the honorable title of professor in my book for his invaluable feedback and friendship; Kaitlyn Beck, my cousin and friend, who once again modeled as Lana for the covers of the spin-off series; Rebecca Frank, who once again designed the most lovely covers; Hollie Jackson, whom I'm so glad will be voicing Lana again for the audiobook editions; and finally, my Grim Readers, many of whom emailed and messaged countless times to request more adventures for Lana. Thank you from the bottom of my heart. This new series would have never happened without your insistence. I hope you're as thrilled as I am to be back in Limbo City!

An extra shoutout to my authorly sister, Justina Dodson, who not only proofread my unfinished draft, but also helped brainstorm sexual salad dressing puns for this particular book and came up with the winning condiment. Thank you, Tinker Bell! Also, stay clear of the salad bar in Duat. Eeep!

If you are as in love with Egypt as I am, I'll be sharing a video tour of the research I did for the gang's travels in my email newsletter and with my Facebook reader group.

www.angelaroquet.com/newsletter
www.facebook.com/groups/angelaroquet

If you're picking this book up well past release but would still like the virtual tour, feel free to email me for the link at **angela@angelaroquet.com**

This has very much been the most fun research I've done for any book, and I'd love to share my favorite notes and links with you!

ABOUT THE AUTHOR

USA Today bestselling author **Angela Roquet** is a great big weirdo. She lives in Missouri with her husband and son in a house stuffed with books, toys, skulls, owls, and glitter-speckled craft supplies. Angela a member of SFWA and HWA, as well as the Four Horsemen of the Bookocalypse, her epic book critique group, where she's known as Death. When not swearing at the keyboard, she enjoys boating with her family at Lake of the Ozarks and reading books that raise eyebrows.

You can find Angela online at
www.angelaroquet.com

If you enjoyed this book, please leave a review or tell a friend. Your support means so much!